RENOVATING THE HEART OF A BEAST

ADDICTED TO A BBW

MASTERPIECE

N. YVONNE PRESENTS

Published by S.Yvonne Presents

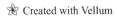

Created with Vellum

SUBSCRIBE

Interested in keeping up with more releases from S.Yvonne Presents? To be notified first on upcoming releases, exclusive sneak peaks, and contest to win prizes. Please subscribe to her mailing list: https://bit.ly/3jKoNbB

SYNOPSIS

Synopsis

Renovating The Heart Of A Beast is a fast pace emotional world wind novel about four different individuals finding themselves betrayed in the name of love.

Meet Praylah a beautiful plus size woman that battles with bipolar and depression. Locked into a toxic relationship with a one-year-old daughter. She learns to navigate through all her pain in suffering. Not knowing your worth as a woman can be detrimental. Praylah still manages to be the sweet soft girl that she is until she meets a man that ends up flipping her world upside down.

Michael aka Debo is charming and very handsome with a list of issues that could be harmful to himself as well as others. When he sets his eyes on a woman that he deems as pure. He doesn't stop at nothing to get her. The only thing is that his own mental is off, and his heart needs to be renovated properly.

Soulful Hurtz, talented football player, taking care of his two younger siblings and feeling as though his life is right where he wants it to be. He married his high school sweetheart and still feels as though something is missing in what was supposed to be his happy ending. Secrets are spilled and betrayal arises. Soulful's heart desperately needs renovation, the only problem is, he has to be open to accept.

Era Smith, chocolate beauty should be her name. She has a beautiful angelic voice and works as a restaurant manager. Things take a turn when her boyfriend Devin snatches her dream of becoming an R&B singer away from her. Feeling betrayed and heartbroken she encounters another problem that she wasn't ready for, Soulful Hurtz.

THANK YOU

Special out to all my loyal readers!

KEEP IN TOUCH

Subscribe

Interested in keeping up with more of my releases? To be notified first of all my upcoming releases and sneak peeks, please subscribe to my mailing list! https://bit.ly/3AYIwMK

Contact me on any of my social media handles as well!

Facebook- Authoress Masterpiece & Masterpiece Reads

Facebook private group for updates- Masterpiece Readers

Instagram- authoress_masterpiece & masterpiece_lgee

Email – masterpiece3541@outlook.com

PRAYLAH

"I'm coming in late today, gotta grind so our lights won't get cut off in the morning."

I rolled my eyes and said nothing, simply hanging up in Jarei's face. I made my baby girl some breakfast then put a towel down in the center of our queen-size bed so she could eat while I showered. Today I had to work a double shift, it was also Valentine's Day so I knew the restaurant would be super busy. I just didn't care to be all in the mix seeing happy couples smile at each other.

I was twenty-six years old with a one-year-old daughter. Besides my parents, I experienced true love with my baby girl. Once upon a time, I thought I had true love with Jarei but that had been proven time and time again that it was hitting on nothing. I often wondered what I was doing and my purpose in life. I worked as a waiter, dropped out of high school only to struggle. My parents kicked me out when I refused to live my life like a good ol' Christian girl.

I was too busy infatuated with Jarei's dog ass and loving him meant everything to me when I was seventeen. Jarei broke me down until I felt like I was nothing. If it wasn't my weight, it was the ugly red and purple birthmark plastered on my face that he constantly despised and made me put on tons of makeup to cover. I had always been awkward looking, my parents always told me that I was unique and very beautiful.

My light apricot skin tone and monolid eyes were often complimented. I had natural red kinky curly hair that I often gave up on and let it do its thing by being free into a big curly fro. I met Jarei walking home from school one day. I was thick back then, wearing a size fourteen. He treated me like I was the most beautiful woman he had ever met. He didn't have much money but had a car and would hustle hard. I grew up spoiled as the only child so I was used to having every and anything that I wanted.

When I decided to go against my parents' wishes for Jarei, I pained my parents bad. My father was a preacher and couldn't take the embarrassment nor the sin I was living in. My momma pleaded and begged him to forgive me and just work with me. Her argument was me dealing with the changes and hormones of becoming a woman. That wasn't good enough for my dad, he put me out and I had no choice but to shack up with Jarei.

At the time his mom was a dope fiend who was never at home. Jarei was twenty-three years older than me at the time, so he became my boyfriend and acted as if he was my father bossing me around and being very controlling. Things took a turn when his mom overdosed and died. I started feeling sorry for him. My love turned into pity. He would have his moments where he would treat me nice, but on most days, he was evil as hell.

If I didn't do what he asked, he would get violent and very physical. Then he would do some physiological shit that always worked on me like Ike did Tina. He always would remind me that I was all that he had, and I knew that was true. It's why I stayed with him, I figured that one day he would get back to the old Jarei and really start loving me.

I really didn't have any friends, besides my best friend Era and my other friend Ju'well. I had a couple of coworkers that I could text here and there. All I knew was my parents and Jarei, and of course I had my one-year-old as well.

I believed Jarei, when it came to all the negative things, he said to me. The more I looked at myself the more uncomfortable I had grown with myself. I was 5'6 now weighing three hundred pounds. My face was round and chubby, I now had a small double chin that I hated looking at.

I didn't get to go around Jarei's friends because he was ashamed of me. Every diet I tried to do, I failed at. I had a c-section with my baby girl and the extra weight just kept coming on top of my baby weight. I once loved my big birthmark, now I hate it and covered it every chance I got.

My stomach tightened from thinking of how Jarei would probably come in swinging since I hung up in his face. I didn't believe shit he said anymore, and he probably was used to coming in late as an excuse to go be with his first baby momma. Speaking of first baby momma, I looked down at my phone and saw that it was her calling.

"Good morning, Nyla." I didn't like arguing or being confrontational with her. She hated me because even though she carried Jarei's firstborn he still chose me but crept around with her. She didn't understand why Jarei had chosen me, and I didn't either. Nyla was slim-thick and beautiful, skin clear from any blemishes.

"Good morning baby momma number two. Happy love day." Nyla loved reminding me how I was the main chick but still came in second when it came time to delivering Jarei's baby. Jarei Jr was two years old, and I loved him to pieces.

His mom and dad were always busy, so he became a big responsibility of mine.

I broke up with Jarei and slept on my parents' couch for about three weeks before my father was back down my throat, ready for me to repent to the Lord and get back in the church. I was broken-hearted and missed Jarei. He wore me down good, hustling hard and buying me gifts, to get me back. Little did he know I had no choice. Soon as I came back home Nyla was there leaving Jr. on our doorstep. I got my ass beat that night because I wasn't ready to step up and watch a baby that crushed me. A baby that didn't belong to me. Jarei broke me down good, and I watched him walk out the door leaving me with his son. He stayed out all night and came home saying he was sorry, and how he was going to get the proper help he needed to help him control his anger.

Five in the morning he made love to me like he wasn't disgusted by the rolls of fat that decorated my body. He kissed me from head to toe and I believed every word he said. That morning we created my baby girl, and he was happy a month later when I told him I was pregnant. A light shined in him, and he stopped putting hands on me only until after I gave birth. That's when the demon in him came back out to play. He started trying his hardest to make my life a living hell. I was always apologizing and trying to strategize a way to make him happy. Hot and cold was the definition of Jarei. Even with my bipolar disorder, I fought tooth and nail to stay sane and make our home as happy as possible. Jarei was heavy in the streets but could never seem to get right at all.

If money was bad on his end, it was left to me to make sure he had some form of re up money. That's why I worked so hard and sacrificed a lot like getting my nails and feet done. I would often try to look like something by pressing my own hair out but that was a hard task. All I cared about was making sure my baby girl had what she needed. I would die before I let my baby girl go without. I kept her with nice clean clothes on and her hair greased up and parted with big bows on the ends.

"Thanks, Ny. Same to you." Then there was that uncomfortable silence. Until she smacked her lips and started demanding things from me like I was her baby's father.

"Anyway Praylah. I need to drop Jr. off today. He will be spending the night with you. I got a Valentine's date and I'm not missing it." I sighed as I watched Heaven, my baby girl, smile wide and sing along with Cocomelon. She hadn't touched her food yet, but I knew soon as I stepped in the shower she would.

"Sorry, Nyla. I have to work a double. I'm paying my cousin to watch Heaven all day until night fall." She smacked her lips; I would take Jr. too but I was already running low on money. My cousin Natasha was very demanding when it came to her money. She took good care of Heaven, but it came with a fee. Also, because she knew of Jarei's cheating on me with Nyla, it was very embarrassing, and I hated hearing Natasha go on and on about how much of a dumb bitch I was. Just to teach me a lesson, Natasha would charge me extra for Jr.

"Doesn't matter Praylah! I'm pulling up already. My hair appointment is in the next thirty minutes. He will be at the front door in seconds." She hung up before I could tell her no. This was Nyla's normal behavior. There was no point in calling her back because she was probably rushing Jr. to my front door now with no baby bag. She played things how she saw fit. She knew that I wouldn't just leave a two-year-old on my doorstep.

I grabbed two dry-off towels and wrapped them around me. I hurried and made my way through the house to reach the front door hoping Heaven didn't get up and make a mess trying to follow me. Just as I thought, Jr. little cute self-stood at the door with his pacifier in his mouth. He smiled while managing to keep his pacifier still in place. His nose was running, and it instantly pissed me off that he didn't have a damn jacket on. When he got sick then Heaven would catch a cold then next was me. Jarei wasn't here long enough to catch wind of the cold, so he always was the lucky one. I looked up and saw Nyla speeding off. Holding out my index finger, Jr. gripped it with his small hand as I helped him inside and led him to the bed with Heaven.

The two of them got along well and were very close. Anxiety began to hit me hard. I didn't want to call Jarei. I was still mad at him. He hadn't been home in two days claiming he was hustling. Today would have to be the day he came home and helped with these kids. I really didn't have the money to pay out for both kids. I had to be at work in the next two hours, so I had to move fast on getting Jarei to cooperate with me and watch his kids. My mind went back to our conversation earlier. He didn't even wish me a Happy Valentine's. It was starting to feel like I was more of his crutch than a girlfriend.

"Bitch, you hung up in my face earlier." I could hear the anger in his voice. He had been waiting on me to call apparently because he picked up on the first ring.

"My phone died, Jarei, I'm sorry." I talked above a whisper. I could never get used to him blatantly calling me out of my name. I never disrespected Jarei so I still couldn't wrap my head around him disrespecting me.

"The fuck you want?" I could hear a couple of voices in his background and knew he was around his homies. Early in the morning, he acted like he couldn't go a minute without being around a bunch of niggas. He was supposed to be hustling, making money but it always sounded like a small get-together in his background. He always came back home with a story about how the streets were moving slow, and he didn't have enough to carry at least half of the bills.

"Umm, Nyla just dropped Jr. off. I have a double to work and I can't afford to pay for him as well." I got straight to the point. I didn't want to waste more time explaining to Jarei how disrespectful his baby's mother was. They both had a lack of consideration when it came to me and what all I had on my plate. I was drained but still found a little push somewhere deep inside of myself to keep going.

"You got to figure that shit out Pray, you already know the deal with me." Before I could find the courage to tell him that it wasn't fair, and this was not my kid technically, he hung up in my face. I stood still in place with tears of frustration in my eyes. This just couldn't be my life. I wish I had more courage, a stronger backbone to stand up for myself.

It often became hard to ignore negative thoughts especially when you battled hard with bipolar disorder. I was at the point of planning an escape. I knew like hell Jarei would give me hell if I told him that I wanted to leave. He probably feared me leaving just because he didn't want to step up and be a father to his other child. He knew that with me I wouldn't ask him for shit when it came to Heaven.

However, Nyla would leave Jr. on him, forcing him to step the fuck up and be a father.

Checking in on the kids, I got sad all over again. They were so innocent and didn't ask to be here. I feared leaving Jr. I mean look at who he had for a mom and dad.

Walking to my bathroom, I opened my medicine cabinet while nibbling on my bottom lip. My depression was at an all-time high and I needed my mood stabilizer medication to keep me balanced for the day. Lithium is what my doctor prescribed me. It worked wonders, it helped control the highs and lows of my disorder. I was also able to recognize when it was my disorder that would have me feeling so down and out and on edge.

I BATTLED with it since a kid, even though I was spoiled it was always that nagging feeling in the back of my brain. I would think that my mere existence wasn't enough. I would feel useless and sometimes miserable with my mania episodes.

SITTING IN THE DARK, putting bruises on my skin and then inflicting pain to feel alive was one of my biggest problems that I tried my best to hide from my parents. Now that I'm grown, I'm happy they got me the proper help and therapy.

HAVING no medical insurance made me get a job to help stay on top of my disorder. I didn't want Jarei seeing or knowing that side of me. Being off my meds would have me purposely starting things with him just to feel the pain he would inflict on me so I wouldn't inflict it on myself. The fucked up way he talked to me while off my meds also had me believing it and feeling so low that at times I battled with taking my own life.

I PRAYED ALL THE TIME, because I had a daughter to raise, and I wanted to be healthy and sane for her. So, I worked my ass off just to keep this medication and continue to pay for refills. Noticing I only had a week's supply left I sighed hard. Once again, all bills were left on me for the month. I liked to have extra spending money to be able to feed me and Heaven.

My food stamps had been cut because they tried to stick me with fraud after finding out that Jarei was fucking my worker and she was purposely giving us more benefits. I prayed that one of my regular good tipping customers was at the restaurant today. They would tip so good that I'd have enough spending money for the entire week.

Pushing my thoughts to the side, I stepped into the shower and said a silent prayer.

MICHAEL AKA DEBO

Nigga you ain't really bout that life! This nigga done passed on you with three fuckin' bricks and he still sitting here pleading his got damn case!

"Shut the fuck up!" I shook my head and blinked my eyes hard.

"Yo Debo, you good nigga?" Solo looked at me like I had lost my mind and I was starting to believe that I was. That was my tenth time hearing that fucking voice in just one week. That fucking voice just kept popping up, cold part about it was for the past year I had been battling tough with it. Solo knew that something was wrong, he just didn't like bringing the shit up. Solo was like a brother to my brother-in-law. So, I knew both of them niggas talked about the weird shit they had been witnessing with me. I didn't give a fuck because I was grown and couldn't no nigga tell me how the fuck to live my life.

"Where the fuck my shit at nigga?" I smashed the gun hard on top of Junebug's forehead, then gleamed at all the blood that spurted from this nigga's head. He had been ducking and dodging my soldiers for the past two weeks. If I had to step down from distribution, then a nigga was going to pay up with his life. I hated tracking niggas down when it came to my money. Although I knew that Ream, my brother-in-law wouldn't snatch my position from me because he knew I was a thoroughbred nigga. I never got too comfortable and slacked off, not even for small shit like this nigga Junebug running my goons in circles trying to locate him for a couple of thousands not even worth the sweat and hassle.

"Debo, listen-" He flinched hard as hell as I made my way directly into his face.

"No nigga, you listen!" *What the fuck he got to listen to Michael? I swear you on some pussy ass shit nigga! Put this niggas brains in his lap and move on to the next nigga!*

"Fuck!" My head was now throbbing and the more I looked up at the bright lights the more I felt like I was about to pass out. I glanced over at Solo and shook my head. He had a look of concern covering his face as I just simply nodded my head toward Junebug.

"I gotta step out for a minute, run to the car. Have a talk with that nigga then end him." I said nothing else; I hurriedly picked my feet up and quickly walked out of the warehouse. My heart painfully beat hard and fast in my chest like I had run a marathon. My ears felt congested as hell as my vision was growing blurry.

I knew I wouldn't hear the last of today's event from Solo. It was nothing for him to handle and end a nigga exactly where he stood but that was my job. Solo only came with me today because he was around the hood collecting bread and decided to ride over here with me. The Blue Diamond Dynasty was a well-organized organization. Although half of our dealings were illegal, we kept shit squared away and tight, never stepping out of our roles to cause any form of confusion.

"Ain't shit a Perc thirty won't fix." I mumbled to myself, picking up my pace to reach my truck. I hopped inside and opened my middle console. I eyed the pills as if my life had depended on them. Popping two in my mouth, I crushed them with my teeth until I felt the strong powder of the pills on my tongue. I quickly chased it down with water and closed my eyes, pacing my breathing.

"Fuck is wrong with me?" I really wanted to know. Lately, that voice that I always thought was my conscience, had been fighting me hard as fuck. It felt like that voice wanted to take over me and control my every move. It often disagreed with a lot of my decision making and just to shut it up, I found myself doing what it said. My father battled hard with mental issues and my sister Mattea had her own personal mental problems that she got under control just like my father.

I really ain't want to go to them with what I thought wasn't serious. They always felt like I needed them to figure out my fucking problems anyway when I didn't. A nigga did so much dark shit in my time span of living that it was starting to eat away at me. This shit was going to pass, and I would be just fine. I just felt abnormal as fuck lately and it was starting to make me lose my cool.

I chose to live a gritty life because that voice led me toward it. It's what made me feel sane. Killing niggas and chasing after my own money is what I was about. I often took the shit too far and would regret it until I convinced myself that it was just fine and that I had to do what I had to do. I didn't like depending on a soul and I damn sure didn't like a person thinking that I needed them for shit. Out of all my father's kids, I probably was the dark child, the one that gave him and my mom the most fucking problems.

I was born into wealth, and I didn't give a fuck since I

was old enough to remember that I didn't give a fuck. I picked my phone up and took a look at all the missed calls and text messages, mainly from my mom and dad. Then my sister Mattea sent me text messages just simply annoyed with my decision to ignore them all.

I missed my family, but they got on my nerves. They didn't respect the fact that I was a grown-ass man. Deep down inside I was also embarrassed, scared that I would flip out at the wrong time and make them disown a nigga. I didn't want that at all because they all were my lifeline. Especially my mom, she just had that soft welcoming touch. That's another reason I stayed away from them. One look at me and my momma would know that something was wrong with me. I didn't need her worrying when my dad and siblings was enough work for her to have to deal with.

I sat stuck for a minute, rolling me up a blunt and sparking it. Inhaling then exhaling, I let the thoughts race through my brain. For the life of me, I couldn't establish who the fuck I was. That in itself would make the average person want to blow their brains out. I didn't even know what the fuck was going on with me, I desperately tried to sort it out but couldn't. Right now, I felt like I had a little bit of control but each day that passed felt like I was losing a grip that could end up dangerous for me and the people surrounding me.

One moment, I got full control over myself and the next I was a raging fuckin' beast ready to annihilate some shit. *Boom! Boom! Boom*! Instead of jumping I pulled my nine and pointed it towards the noise. Seeing it was Ream, I rolled the window down and looked at him.

Ignoring the rage that was hidden behind his eyes I waited for him to speak.

"Nigga you on that trippy shit again. Go get you some

help my nigga." Taking my time to light my blunt, I stepped out of the car. I was sick of grown-ass niggas looking at me like they were worried or some shit.

"Nigga you sound like my fuckin' sister. That's why I'm ignoring them folks. Ain't shit wrong with me." I cracked my neck, taking a long pull from my blunt. I checked out the surroundings and then focused back on Ream.

"Them folks? You saying that shit like they not ya family nigga." His nose flared as he stepped a little closer. *Knock this nigga the fuck back!* Why weren't the pills doing their job, I wondered, ignoring the voice. "Fuck all that, Solo shot me a text saying you left it up to him to do yo job."

"I ain't fenna stand here nigga explaining to you or that snitching nigga what the fuck I'm on. Nigga I needed some fucking air, get off my dick! Since you came all the way out here to check up on me, you go in there and finish the shit along with him." I was livid, so livid that before I found myself doing some more way-out shit, I turned my back on Ream and jumped back into my car.

"Aye Debo, you my wife little brother and I love you, nigga. Next time you talk to me out of pocket, my beautiful wife gone be turning back into Reaper dressed in all black hunting me down for killing her stupid ass baby brother. Tighten up nigga." He stood there like he was daring me to say some shit. Little did he know I was feeling super challenged right now. I was fighting something super strong inside of my body. That voice was screaming out loud in my head and right now I felt like it was trying to take over, like I was close to having an outer body experience. If I gave in something bad was bound to happen, for one Ream just challenged and threatened me. That demon inside of me didn't take too kind to that shit.

I smirked at him and started up my car, speeding the fuck

off. I had major love for Ream and Solo, the main thing I needed them niggas to understand now was that I was grown. I didn't need them trying to be my fuckin' guardians. I was the boss and the leader of myself, I didn't need no nigga including my father to hold my nuts while I took a piss.

I was no longer that stupid ass young wild nigga that did shit just for a reaction or to satisfy my thirst. At twenty-eight years old I paved my own fuckin' way from owning businesses and holding shit down on my own. They needed to respect me and stop questioning and acting like they were a niggas master. Shit I had a dad, and that nigga was overbearing. Shit just kept triggering me and soon that shit wouldn't be safe for niggas health.

* * *

* * *

Pulling up to my favorite restaurant that I owned, I parked right in the front not even turning the engine off, I left the keys right in the ignition for the valet to take over.

Looking up at my restaurant "Beastly Cravings" I felt a small calm take over me. I was high as hell feeling the effects of the Percocet's. As long as that voice was fucking quiet, I was fine with that. It was something about coming here that gave me a certain peace that I couldn't explain. I loved eating and cooking in my downtime, which was why I put my money into some shit that I loved to do.

Beastly Cravings was a franchise that I had started in California. Once one restaurant got big because of the top-of-the-line steaks and seafood that we specialized in, I started the franchise and moved it around to different states.

Soon, I was going to have to back down all the way from the streets and focus on my business. I already knew Ream and Solo had been having side conversations about a nigga, wondering about my capability to still run with them in the dynasty. I had my own back up plan. I actually planned on stepping down by the age of thirty. I had so much money already saved up from my franchises alone that if I truly wanted to, I could retire now.

To keep it real, I didn't know how bad this hearing voices and losing control shit was going to get. The streets were good for two reasons. That was making money and taking niggas souls when I felt on edge or when they disrespected the code. Lately, my judgment had been off, and having to kill a nigga today for coming up short was a prime example of me feeling like I was starting to lose my touch with this street shit.

I took a seat in the back of my restaurant, no one even knew that I was the owner and I kept it that way. I didn't want anyone faking and laying it on thick when the owner popped up. The only person that knew of me owning this place was the woman that I had running this joint. Era Smith, her work ethic was sick, and she stayed on top of everything concerning this specific restaurant. I often rotated her to the other local Beastly Cravings but since this was the busiest one, I kept her here mainly.

I didn't know much about her, from what I looked into with her, she was still chasing her dreams of becoming a singer. She had a good-ass resume when I interviewed her back at my big ass office which served as my franchise head-quarter. Era didn't fold under pressure and running a five-star restaurant came with ups and downs. I interviewed her right along with my board and she sold herself so good that I let her be over hiring and managing other managers at my other locations. Whenever Era had a new idea or new ingredient, I let her do her thing. She had the numbers at my restaurants looking good and that's why I rocked hard with her and kept her pockets laced.

Since I was over on the Eastside, I decided to shoot my boy Sosa a text to have him come meet with me while I was over in his neck of the woods. Sosa was my nigga, only difference was we didn't come up the same way, but we crossed paths in the streets and in jail back when I was really causing havoc in the streets. Under the Blue Diamond Dynasty, I had my own crew that I ran with an iron fist.

My gang was known as the Slaughter Gang Niggas. All my niggas were really like that and had muthafuckas fearing and respecting them all in one. Sosa's gang were known as M.G.N *Money Getting Niggas.* They were just as cold as my Slaughter Gang Niggas. We clicked up often when it came time to doing hood tournaments and making niggas place high bets on our street football team. I wanted to plan some big shit for my birthday and put my skills to the test. Back in high school I was that nigga when it came to football.

I enjoyed coaching niggas and placing high bets to make bread off the sport alone. Snapping me out of my thoughts both of my phones started to ring at the same damn time. Ignoring my business line, I looked down at my personal line and noticed it was Alesia my business assistant calling. I ignored her call only because I was in a shitty mood and didn't want to snap off on her.

Alesia was demanding as fuck but also smart. She was one of those broads that took her job too fucking serious, often forgetting who the fuck paid and signed her checks. Five seconds later my personal phone started ringing again. I got queasy just looking at the name flash across my screen, Lakendra. *Ignore her pitiful ass!* Answering the call even though I didn't want to answer her, I did anyway. Always feeling guilty as fuck when it came to her.

"What's good ma?" I looked at my watch and frowned. I was gon' have to pull Era to the side. It should never take a waiter in my restaurant more than five minutes to approach the table.

"Hey Bo. I wanted to know if you were coming home tonight. I wanted to cook for you and watch some movies." Holding in the deep breath that I took I didn't want to sigh hard into the phone and hurt Lakendra's feelings. People from the outside looking in felt as though I didn't owe her shit. I felt like I owed her ass a whole lot.

I put her through some dark shit that I still haven't forgiven myself for. Lakendra could be very sweet but also provoking as fuck when things didn't go how she wanted them to.

"Yea, I'll be there later on. Make some tacos and pick out a movie, Ken." I wanted to remind her for the millionth time that we weren't together. That would just start an argument and I didn't need any triggers for the rest of the day. In a couple of months, I planned on moving out of me and Lakendra's five-bedroom house and copping me some other shit. I just couldn't leave her high and dry. I took the shit day by day trying to help this girl figure out what she wanted to do in life so I could finance whatever it was and move on with my life.

"Okay Bo! I'm excited now, I've been missing you." She cooed in the phone and my stomach dropped. I hadn't touched Lakendra in months because I didn't want to confuse her ass.

"Bet." I hung up on her not waiting for her to respond. I wasn't going home no time soon; I powered off my second line and scanned the restaurant one more time.

"Hello sir, my name is Praylah. I will be your waiter for this evening." I fooled around with my phone not giving her any attention or acknowledgment until I realized that she was late getting around to my table. I pierced her with my eyes, right when she was sitting down my cold glass of water. Our eyes connected and she fumbled the glass acting like she knew me or was all of a sudden starstruck.

The cold ice water caused me to jump out of my seat. I was waiting for that voice to talk to me, but it never came. I could feel my jaws clenching tight as I stared hard at her with a pensive stare. Fear was evident in her eyes now; I could see her hands shaking hard as she snatched up some napkins into her small hands and slowly approached me.

"Sir, I am so sorry… I, umm, never saw a man with eyes like yours and they kind of umm, caught me by surprise." My anger started slipping away the longer she stood there in front of me all timid and shit. She was short but had crazy curves, the kind of curves that came straight from down south. If she wasn't from the dirty dirty then she definitely just had a baby who helped spread her hips wide.

She had that prissy soft girl shit going on with her. The only thing I didn't like was all that fucking make up and pretty curly red hair covering up most of her face. Her curly fro was so big, I frowned at the fact that her ass ain't have anything covering her head while serving folks their food. Yea, Era was gon' hear from me ASAP. I didn't need any bad reviews on my establishment because of this ditzy ass pretty bitch.

I grabbed the napkins out of her trembling hands then enclosed my whole hand on top of hers. Raising my brows and licking my lips, I gave her a tight smile.

"Why you so fuckin' nervous." Her eyes got wide, I guess from me calling her out.

"I, ummm-" She tried to retrieve her hand from mine, but I tightened my grip. I almost found myself laughing with how fucking scared she was acting. Then again, she should have every right to be scared. She was in the presence of a cold-blooded killer. I killed people for lesser fuck ups.

"Calm the fuck down and stop saying umm and shit. You acting real skittish and I don't like that." Just to fuck with her, I rubbed my thumb over the top of her soft-ass hand. That's the real reason why I hadn't loosened my grip. Her hands were so fucking soft that it felt like silk. My thoughts were getting the best of me because I was ready to press her for those digits but realized that I couldn't be fraternizing with bitches that worked for me.

I released her hand and I saw her take in a deep breath and quickly walk the fuck away. Shaking my head, I had the right mind to stomp back there and snatch Era up and ask her why the fuck did she have this bitch working at my restaurant. Not wanting to make a big deal about shit, I waited for Era to come behind the redhead and apologize for her actions.

While Era could be seen coming from the back where the chefs prepared all the food at, I shook my head in satisfaction because she was already bringing out my favorite meal. Steak with lobster and mashed potatoes with my secret sauce that I created years ago. The same sauce that had my competitors coming to sit and dine just to figure out my ingredients.

Mr. Brownston, my deepest apologies, sir." I liked how when we were out in the open, Era kept shit professional. "I have some good news." She leaned close and talked low. Era looked like a black Barbie doll. Her skin was close to being pitch black but flawless. Every single feature on her was perfect as hell and she was a beautiful curvy voluptuous chick. Sexually I wasn't attracted to her, but I always acknowledged and told her how beautiful she was.

I knew deep down and real soon Era was going to make it big with her singing shit. She sounded like a fucking angel.

"NFL player Soulful Hurtz rented out the entire restaurant. I should have the dates provided soon." I smiled at that and forgot all about even being mad about the water being spilled all over me. Soulful was my boy. I met him at the last super bowl and thanked his ass for putting millions in my pockets from betting high on him. I told him all about the street team I had and in his free time he would come down and watch and give my coaches some tips.

Soulful was a real down-to-earth street nigga that still kept shit a hunnid. I had nothing but respect for the young nigga. He had a hard life growing up and wasn't ashamed of none of that shit. What made it even better was that he didn't even know he was supporting my franchise by showing his face here. I don't even think the nigga knew that this shit was mine.

Before I could respond back to what it was, I had to say Sosa was walking up with a big ass smirk on his face. Era eyed him and kind of rolled her eyes on the sly. I never saw her act that way towards anybody, so I wondered if my boy was smashing her.

"I'll have another waiter come up and serve y'all. Call me later so I can run a new menu by you first." She offered that soft smile as Sosa took a seat ignoring Era like he had no clue why she was suddenly giving him the stank face.

"I got you, and I think I want you to fire redhead. She too fuckin' ditzy."

"She's just having a bad day; I can reassure you that she will be better next time. Mr. Brownston." Deciding not to get on Era tough, I allowed her to walk away. I slapped hands hard with Sosa. I pointed to the back of Era and raised my brows as Sosa shrugged and playfully chanted Chief Keef's song. Nigga swore he was really like that.

"These bitches love Sosa! O end or no end!" I shook my head and offered his nutty ass a crooked smile.

"The fuck is up nigga?" This was my dog, we both stayed so busy that when we did cross paths, we liked to celebrate each other's success. It was never like me to count the next niggas pockets but with my ear down to the streets Sosa was supposedly getting money, or so I thought. One of my Generals put a bug in my ear about the nigga. I just had to hear it from the horse's mouth before I believed anything.

"Shit, out here making it happen. You already know." I used my thumb and index finger to pull at my beard hairs as I eyed him seriously.

"My nigga, Honor been telling me that you been needing that work from the slaughter gang niggas. Now if you in a bind nigga, I can front you a brick or two half price, but that's it. You know I ain't with the handouts." I brought that up first before we caught up about other shit like the football games, we both planned out yearly. My General was an ill ass bitch that always kept shit a buck with me. Honor said that she ran across Sosa at the club months back and he told her he needed to do some business with me. A nigga like Sosa didn't come to me for shit regarding drugs because he had his own connections. I already figured the nigga must have taken a hit and needed a handout or help with some shit.

The only thing with that is, I didn't give a fuck how cool I was with a nigga. Every man had to figure they own shit out. Since Sosa was my nigga, I decided to let him come to me on his own and I'd tell him face-to-face what I had on my mind regarding the situation. Niggas knew that my meaning of fronting some shit came with a hefty fuckin' price.

"Man, that dike ass bitch doesn't know what she talking bout. I don't need any help like that; it's just our distributor has been trying to knock us over the head with interest fees." He looked at me briefly and then placed his focus on the new waiter that came to the table.

He placed his order and then looked back at me.

"Man, I'm just trying to cop my girl a bigger house and eat a lil more. Work with cha boy." I nodded my head and cut into my steak. I already peeped game; I was gon' work with Sosa, but he just proved to me that he was struggling. A nigga that was really getting it didn't too much care about the price of the work but the quality.

I entertained the nigga a little longer before I got up and stretched. Deciding to hit the club and hang out a little longer with my nigga Sosa, I told him to meet me at one of my favorite strip clubs. *You gon' have to kill that nigga!* I shook my head and sparked a cigarette soon as I got outside waiting for valet to bring my Bugatti to the front of Beastly Cravings. That voice was really starting to agitate the fuck out of me now. I just hoped it didn't fuck with my judgment when it came time to take care of business.

SOULFUL HURTZ

"Did you have to wear all that pink to my game man?" I chuckled at Roberto and his entourage. I didn't care that he came to my game so flamboyant, he was like a big brother to me. Always there when I needed him the most, especially when I lost my mom five years ago to a drug overdose. Roberto, Sovereign, and Inferno had become my family and was there no matter their busy schedule and I was forever grateful to have them every step of the way.

Roberto clapped his hands super loud and one of his security guards handed him over a portable pink fan. Moving his imaginary hair out of his face he batted his long false lashes.

"Did ju have to have me on the front line amongst common folk? I tell ju, I wanted sky box seats. I don't want a body tan until di summer." He talked in his thick Spanish accent, but never missed a beat checking his surroundings. No matter what the blogs assumed and said, Roberto flew in for every game of mine, confusing people. One moment he was dressed like a real ass nigga then the next he'd be wearing pink, his favorite color.

First the blogs would say Roberto was my secret lover until I introduced him to a couple of peers as family. Then they connected the dots and somehow tied him to Mexico. I told him to fall back on coming to so many games. I didn't want the feds looking into him. He rolled his eyes hard at that shit and still came anyway claiming he was the law and that the federales couldn't touch a piece of hair on his skin.

Roberto seemed super chill and nice as fuck to the people outside of his close-knit circle. The cartel knew him as being a deadly monster that didn't take excuses or disrespect to say the least. His father ended up retiring and letting Roberto take the throne following in his father's shoes, but worse Roberto ended up being the cause of a lot of other head cartel men heads being cut off along with their bodies thrown in ditches.

He married a woman that was just as deadly as him and don't ask me how it was possible that he got himself a husband too. Even though he had a man and a woman he still messed around openly with different people. I never dug too deep into that shit because I didn't care to know. He spoiled my sisters and sent gifts and money even though I was already rich monthly, Roberto never gave none of us space to breathe properly and miss him. He used his private jet almost every week to fly back and forth. His security would beat on the door and Roberto would be standing at the front door with his hands on his hips and all the theatrics would begin from there.

Inferno tried to question if he was handling business properly because he seemed to have a lot of downtime on his hands. Apparently, Roberto handled his shit, from what I could see, he stayed on the phone, texting or talking in his native tongue. He and Queen were tight as hell, and I liked that especially for Queen. She was a good mother to her three kids but in her down time when she wasn't tending to her multiple clinics and staying on top of all her business. She would fly down to Mexico to be with Roberto and if Roberto was already down here, we all hung out together.

A lot of my teammates wanted to be cool but since I came from the streets and constantly watching my back and not trusting muthafuckas. I kept a good distance. I had my own family and my sisters stayed up to shit the older they got. Mainly Luv who was now eighteen, Passion was sixteen and super sweet but sneaky. Passion didn't take my mom's death to hard, but Luv did. She still had her moments where she would act out because of it.

In a fucked up way, I felt a little relieved. I missed my mom don't get me wrong and hate that she died the way that she did. She hurt me so much that I felt a great ounce of relief knowing that she couldn't hurt or disappoint me or my sisters. Getting our hopes up, making us think that she would get better and stay in a rehab, if not for me then her two young daughters but she never followed through.

Just a bunch of broken promises that broke me as a man. It took me years to even establish the type of confidence that I now had. It didn't mean that I was a hundred percent good. I had it all now, a wife with no kids, and two siblings that I took good care of like they were mine. Quite often, I felt myself being ungrateful. It's like I couldn't pinpoint what exactly was wrong with me. I had Sovereign, and her kids along with Roberto still I felt like I was missing something.

"Where is that wife of yours?" I shook my head as we walked toward my locker room. I was pretty sure it was empty by now. Whenever we won a game, I stayed on the field talking and celebrating another victory. I was a quarter-back; the pressure was always high whenever I played a game. I felt like I carried my team on my back and they depended on me more than the coach.

"I don't even know; you know Jocelyn loves to shop and do her own thing." I shrugged it off not trying to give it too much thought. Deep down I was angry and tired of making excuses for the woman that I had fell in love with six years ago. I kept trying with Jocelyn because I didn't want to give up on her. Even when I wasn't a hundred percent at my best, I pushed my shit to the side to be a husband to her. Jocelyn lost her brother Havoc around the same time that I lost my mom.

We reconnected and we were there for each other, emotionally and physically. I made her my wife three years ago because I didn't see myself with anyone but her. She turned to alcohol but promised me she would stay away from it because she knew how I felt about addiction. I knew a marriage wasn't supposed to be perfect but most of the time I wasn't so sure if Jocelyn even deserved the dignity of being called a wife. I wasn't no nagging ass worrisome nigga, so I let her do her thing. We both grew up not having much so I knew that she was thrilled about us being super rich and having things. I just wondered how long would she be thrilled and start calming down instead of being out every other day spending money like it was going out of style.

When I felt like I was at the very edge of the world, I pulled myself away and regrouped by myself. Yet when it was the same for my wife, I was the one wrapping my hands around her and pulling her away to show her that we both could get through anything together.

"Hmmm, shopping and splurging she can do that any day out the week. She chooses to do that on a game day? I don't like it, and when are y'all having kids again? I thought two years ago you guys were going to go at it." Walking down the empty hallway, I felt my chest constrict a little from all the adrenaline I had out on the field. It felt like my body was trying to calm itself and just the thought of my wife being non-supportive sent me back into overdrive.

Over the years, I overcame so much shit. Anxiety and depression and a whole lot of pretending like I was good when I really wasn't. I did the best I could and never made excuses for how I felt. I wouldn't dare crumble in front of Jocelyn because I didn't want her thinking that I was some weak nigga that was always emotional.

I did all my crying and talking about my struggles inside my head. When it got to be too much, I would end up expressing myself a little to Sovereign or Roberto. They both were very protective when it came to me, so I held a lot of shit in. I didn't want them not liking Jocelyn and make shit uncomfortable for her when she came around, so I never went to Sovereign specifically when it came to my marriage problems.

Roberto was a little different, he couldn't stand Jah, but he still respected her whenever she was around, and I appreciated that. He didn't like her because he saw firsthand how she moved selfishly, not considering the people around her. I never put too much on her, I didn't even expect her to help with my sisters because they weren't her responsibility. Even that shit was starting to become strange.

"She told me that she didn't want to have kids until Passion was eighteen, so I guess we got two more years." Roberto smacked his lips hard.

"Thissss Chica is a special kind of wife. You okay with that?" He folded his arms and started tapping his foot. You could hear the echo of his foot traveling down the hallway.

"I guess I have to be. I mean shit, a marriage is about coming to common grounds and sacrificing. If she don't want my kids right now then I got to wait, plus I'm knee deep with football. I'm trying to win the super bowl again this year." I smiled hard at that. My accomplishments really made me feel good about myself.

"Every time I creep up on you two, you both seem to be plotting some shit. Teddy, let me find out you trying to make side deals with Berto's cartel." I turned to Sovereign's voice and smiled like a kid in the candy store. Sovereign had an aura to her that just automatically brought you comfort. Sometimes I found myself looking at her like the mother and big sister I wish I had. Her heels clicked against the floors as she moved closer with Inferno always trailing a couple feet back with his eyes glued to her backside.

Stevie Wonder himself could see how bad these two had it for each other. Her perfume overpowered any other smells surrounding us. I gave her a big hug and slapped hands with Inferno.

"Good game, my boy. Y'all fasho winning Superbowl this year. I'm dropping big money on it." I nodded my head because I was confident that this year belonged to the Packers.

"Well, let's all meet at your house Teddy. I been trying to catch up with Luv. I've been calling her for three days now to get her to watch the kids for Inferno and I. We supposed to be going on vacation this weekend. I texted her ass and asked and she told me she'd let me know." Sovereign giggled but I didn't find shit funny about it. Luv ain't have shit to do and it wouldn't and shouldn't be a problem with the kids coming through for her to sit and watch them.

"Yea, we can do dinner at my house. I'll call Jah and let her know. You already know I got the kids though; you didn't even have to text to ask Luv ass." I couldn't wait to catch up with my own little sister myself. She was in and out of the house every chance she got. She was supposed to be going to a community college for cosmetology and told me that it was what she was doing that kept her busy. I just wasn't sure if her ass was being honest.

Like I said, Luv gave me the most problems. Passion was graduating early and going to Birmingham on a scholarship. Luv opted out of going to a university. She claimed that she wanted something different, so I respected her.

"I'll catch up with y'all later. My ice bath is waiting for me." We all said our farewells until later. As I made my way to the locker room, I stripped down leaving my cleats by the bench. I walked towards the huge ice tub with my phone in my hands. The first person I called was my wife as I eased into the freezing water. Once my body was immersed in it, I let out a low grumble. Jocelyn didn't answer and I wasn't feeling that shit. So, I waited until my body went numb inside the tub then dialed her again.

"Hey babe, what's up?" I remained quiet for a while listening to her loud ass background. Pulling at my chin hairs to calm myself I couldn't find the right words.

"I hate when you do that Soulful. You called me and yet you're not talking." Clearing my throat, I held the phone tighter.

"I'm trying to figure out why the fuck it sounds like you out at a club or somewhere when I had a football game today." Thinking about the conversation that me and Roberto had, I could feel myself becoming pissed the fuck off.

"Since when did you care about me making your games?" She smacked her lips and chuckled.

"I shouldn't want you to do shit. You should want to support me, like I'm always doing for you." This was the shit I didn't like, she never had to tell me how the fuck to be a husband. Yet, I stayed hinting around to her how to be a fucking wife.

"I went out shopping with my girls and they wanted to get drinks afterwards. Nothing major, Soulful. I'll be home before you get there, I got some sexy ass lingerie that I plan on wearing for you tonight, to celebrate your victory. I already know my big daddy won." That caused me to smile and forget about even being mad with her.

"Yea alright, but I need you to start supporting a nigga more. That shit look bad as fuck, not that I give a fuck what muthafuckas think. You just never around when it comes to the shit that's important as fuck to me. We having company tonight, so I need you to cook up some shit and make sure the house straight." I counted down to five, I already knew she was getting ready to bitch.

"Why not mention this in advance Soulful? I wasn't in the mood for company."

"You in the mood to shop and shit. Wanna be seen so fuckin' bad with them hoe ass bitches. Aye Jah, you slipping the fuck up again. Tighten the fuck up and watch yo self." I threatened and hung the fuck up in her face. I appeared like a nice ass nigga because I was always nonchalant about shit and very easy going.

One thing I wasn't was a pussy ass nigga. I was getting tired of Jocelyn acting like she didn't know what the fuck I was about. I didn't ask much of her and didn't even require her to do anything as my wife but cook and fuck a nigga good. It was my fault that she was probably this lazy because I spoiled her just like I did my sisters. I made enough money that I gave everybody in my household options. Jocelyn didn't have to lift a finger. She wasted so much money investing in shit she never carried out.

I didn't complain or make her do anything that she was

uncomfortable doing. I was tired of her excuses and hearing the same ol' same ol'. Jocelyn needed to step it up a little or our marriage would be in the danger zone. If I didn't put up with my own momma shit, then I wasn't gon' put up with a wife that could never show up for a nigga.

ERA

It felt like mountains were looming over my heart. I stood close to the door watching and listening to my so-called producer boyfriend pound the lining out of his artist's pussy. My breathing became more and more shallow because, for the life of me, I didn't understand just where we went wrong.

Feeling myself grow weak by the second, I swallowed a lack of spit and focused in on the way he eyed her. Devin looked at this woman like she was the only woman for him. I don't even think I ever felt him in the way that he was fucking her.

"Past five minutes." Tears slowly ran down my face as I caught and backhanded them. He couldn't fuck me past two minutes, yet he was sitting in there giving that bitch the best that he had. I don't know why I was planted the way that I was. I couldn't move, and I didn't really even want to make myself seen.

I picked my heart and pride off the floor, took a couple of pictures of his lying conniving ass, and walked away back towards my car.

I would never fight another bitch just because my man couldn't give me the same respect and loyalty that I gave him for the past three years.

I didn't ask Devin for shit, yet, I always went above and beyond to please, satisfy and make him feel like a king. I didn't nag and we both were content with not living together although most thought it was absurd.

Pulling off and out of the parking lot, I dialed my mom and hit my vape like it was a blunt.

"Hey baby." My mother always had a way of making me feel better just by hearing her voice.

"Earlene! That's yo second time burning my scalp!" I chuckled because that voice belonged to my uncle Benny. He was still a pimp, and my mom was a beautician. Uncle Benny was a triplet brother, after him it was Uncle Lenny then Uncle Denny. Uncle Benny was the only bad ass out of all four siblings my mother included. His hair was long as hell and he had my mom press it out for him every two weeks claiming he couldn't trust his hoes touching his hair.

"Shut ya ass Benny." I giggled and sniveled a little, back-handing the tears from my face.

"Devin is cheating on me, Ma." My voice broke again. I hated being this emotional but the feeling of being betrayed with proof so crystal clear in my face was a hard thing to accept.

"Well baby, I told you that. You and Praylah just keep dealing with these men that's not good for your mental or ya health. Now come pick ya momma up from the salon so I can go home and get my deuce deuce. He got you crying, and I done told you if the nigga ever had you calling me sounding all sad, that I was gon' bust a cap in his ass." I could hear the anger in my momma's voice. Although I wanted to pick her up and let her do her thing.

I knew I couldn't I was a grown ass woman and needed to learn to handle my problems without my momma taking the lead.

"I told her ass to leave that nigga alone, we ain't raise her to be no sucker ass lollipop getting sucked on by one of LA's biggest tricks." My Uncle Benny swore that Devin was a trick and that he wasn't going to take me far with my music career. I didn't depend on Devin to do such a thing. It's the main reason why I didn't move in with him or depend on him like he asked me too.

I gave Devin too much space, I just never wanted him thinking that because he was some big-time producer that I wanted him for other reasons. Years ago, he chased me down after a talent show that I had won. From that point on we became close, and he constantly promised to get my mixtapes out there so a big record company could pick me up and sign me. It never happened, in fact he constantly bragged about getting other people deals like the bitch that I just caught him fucking.

"Hush Benny, what good example have you set for her? Out here pimping them girls and being out in them streets." I hung up because I hated hearing them go back and forth. I loved my mom and all three of my uncles dearly with no judgment. What my Uncle Benny did for work was wrong, but he wasn't one of those evil pimps beating on his women.

I looked at it more like some escort shit, he had high-priced hoes. He led them toward celebrities and hosted big parties. At fifty-one my uncles still looked good and carried themselves well. My father was close to Benny, they stopped being friends when he ended up deserting my mom and me. My uncle couldn't respect a man that didn't take care of his responsibilities.

I heard from my father maybe two to three times a year. I

probably saw him once every couple of years. Shit didn't bother me much now, coming up as a kid it bothered me on special holidays. My uncle was always there to make things better, so I never had much time to get depressed over it. It didn't stop me from questioning myself as a kid. I used to wonder why I wasn't special enough for my dad to try to stick around.

Even as an adult, I made no excuses for his poor choices as a father. I felt like I was his responsibility and even if he didn't want my mom, he should have still wanted me since I didn't ask to be here.

I made it to my two-bedroom apartment and immediately slid out of my shoes. Feeling defeated like I wasted an entire off day, I removed my clothes at my front door and let them sit there instead of picking them up to take them to the hamper. Snapping my bra off, I kept my panties on and let my breast hang free. I hated wearing bras and right now, I was agitated by clothes, and the nagging pain from the wired bra added to that. I needed to feel free with no barriers.

Going into my kitchen in nothing but my panties, I snatched my bottle of Stella Rose and unscrewed the top. I thought about calling Praylah but lately, she had her own list of problems, and I didn't want to weigh her down with mine. I ran me some bath water and sipped straight from my wine bottle. Finally getting inside of my tub, I let my tears fall down my face freely.

I was tired, life was back getting the best of me again. It seemed like no matter how good things seemed to be going they ended up eventually going wrong. I refused to give up on myself. I was now twenty-five years of age, and my music hadn't taken off yet. I didn't get lucky like most chicks did and I knew a part of the problem was because of my weight.

I wasn't sloppily fat, but I was considered plus sized. I

had wide and thick hips, a pear-shaped ass, and some heavy breast that caused my back to hurt throughout the day. I had cellulite and stretchmarks, but I knew that I was beautiful. I caught men and women constantly staring at me like I was a work of art since I was old enough to remember.

I had good energy, and I offered my good energy to people that didn't even deserve it half the time. The main person I connected the most with was my best friend Praylah because she was just as sweet as me. I was a bit wilder and more outspoken than her.

The music industry wanted video vixen chicks with BBLs and preferably fair skin. I was dark like midnight itself; my skin was a smooth dark chocolate free of blemishes. I was far from insecure when it came to my size and the tone of my skin. My mother and uncles made sure of that and constantly spoke confidence right into me.

With my shoulders slumped; I pushed my hands under the water then ran them across my face. Devin had me feeling dead inside and hating myself for giving him a chance to overlook all the red flags. Cursing myself because I knew my pressed hair was now waving up since I hadn't wrapped it, my phone rung and I saw that it was Devin calling. This was the norm for him, he'd call and text me all day like he couldn't live without me.

Instead of answering I pressed decline and sent him the pictures that I snapped of him back at the studio. I cried even harder staring at the pictures as proof again of how much he really didn't love me. Silly fucking me, head over hills for a nigga that barely even brought me around his crew. At first, I thought it was because of my weight when I called him out about that he denied it fast. Saying he wanted to protect me, he even used manipulative words by using my own words against me.

Claiming that he supported me and didn't want people in the industry to think that I slept my way to the top by dating him, I didn't know what was real or fake at this point with him. Catching the man you love fucking somebody else was one of the most sickest things to experience. Especially when you deem a man as yours.

When you accept a nigga for who they are. Like when his dick is average and about five inches long, he can't even go round for round or last for that matter in the bedroom. You don't give a fuck because you end up liking and loving him for who he is beside the dick. You take all of a nigga imperfections and level with them because he's your man and you become appreciative for who you ended up with.

So, at times like this when a nigga that ain't even working with a good package deal fucks you over it makes you sick to the stomach. I was mad at myself for even feeling this hurt and distraught about the shit, but I couldn't help the feelings I had for Devin. We were both comfortable with each other. No matter how wrong he was, I wouldn't dare embarrass myself by going on a rant via social media exposing who he truly was.

I never understood why men and women did that. Men would get on Facebook or Instagram and bash their exes saying how they pussy smelled or how a female wasn't clean or didn't take care of their kids like that type of shit wasn't a reflection of who they were as a man. Why would you date a funky dirty broad that didn't take care of their kids?

Same for women that dissed their men for having small dicks and dirty drawers. Like come on sis, you loved that small ass dick and his dirty ass drawers. I got out the tub and ignored my phone that was now ringing like fucking crazy and went to step inside of the shower to scrub my body down.

I got out of the shower, dried off then stared at myself in

the bathroom mirror. My eyes were bloodshot red and puffy. I vowed to myself to never go through another heartbreak like this again and have more discernment when it came time to picking niggas and falling for them. Lathering my body down with baby oil and Baby Magic, I put on some boy shorts and a sports bra then sprayed myself Champagne Toast all over my body.

I doubled back to my living room to pick up my clothes that I lazily threw down and stopped right in the hallway seeing Devin stupid ass sitting on the couch. Hating that I even gave him a key I walked fully into the living room and took a seat right across from him. We both had keys to each other's houses, but we never used them.

Devin hardly came to my apartment, always claiming it was too cramped and small for him. So, I always did the honors and went to his house. Not caring with how crazy I probably looked right now, I stared right at him. I couldn't even believe he had the balls to show up unannounced to plead any kind of case when all the proof was right on those pictures that I took.

I kept telling myself to remain cool, I wasn't going to give him the satisfaction even though right now I wanted to run across my living room and fuck him up. Devin was tall and medium built; he was very attractive. Those green eyes and the waves dipping in his head made women stop and stare at him no matter where we were.

He had the gift of gab and was smooth as hell, he thought about everything he said before he said it. His nonchalant demeanor could drive any sane woman crazy.

"Let's not overreact, Era." His deep voice bounced off my apartment walls. I chuckled lowly giving him a disgusted look. I didn't know what to say without coming off nasty, so I remained silent. I let him have the floor because when he was done, I was making things perfectly clear that we were over.

"I fucked up, a lot of real niggas fuck up especially when you paid, handsome, and well established. Bitches throw themselves at me a lot, you know that you saw proof of that when I take you out. Today out of all the years that we have been dating, I slipped up and caved in." He licked his pink lips like he was lubricating all the bullshit that spilled from his lips.

"We can and will move forward from this baby, you know I love you so much, Era. Damn baby, please don't sit there quietly, say something to me. I'm hurting badly because I hurt you. I'll do anything to fix it, just tell me what that something is." This time my emotions got the best of me, I couldn't stop the tears falling from my eyes.

Why couldn't Devin be the man for me, I really did love him. All the things I confided to him about. Our connection in the beginning was out of this world making me feel like we were truly meant for each other. He hurt me to my core, and I wish what happened today had never happened. He stood from the couch, adjusting his basketball shorts. Pulling up his fresh white tee, he tossed it on the sofa and walked towards me smelling like men's soap and cologne.

He had the nerves to shower before coming here and was even bolder to think that I was about to let him fuck me. I cried a little harder for how much of a dumb bitch he thought I was. Squatting down between my legs, he brought both of my hands inside of his and softly kissed the backs of the both of them.

"I truly love you and can't imagine myself without me… I mean." Clearing his throat and chuckling nervously he corrected his jumbled words. "I can't picture life without you, Era." He squeezed my hand tighter.

"Then why did you fuck us up, Devin? Why did you fuck her?" There was no excuse that he could possibly say to me right now that would get me to forgive him. I had already conditioned my brain to get over him, which was why my heart felt heavy as hell and I couldn't stop the tears. Soon as I got him out of my apartment, I planned on changing my locks the next day and getting a new phone number.

"I fucked up baby. She kept coming on to me, then she just pulled my dick out, start sucking and I couldn't back down. I'm a man Era, and sometimes us men have weaker moments then y'all women." I bit into my bottom lip so hard that I tasted blood. I refrained from slapping the shit out of him.

"Just tell me what I got to do, so we can get past this. I know your trust is going to be fucked up for a while with me, but I am willing to rebuild that for us and prove to you that I can be faithful. I will even move in here with you. So, Era… tell me what it is I gots to do."

"You can just get the fuck out. I don't ever want to see or hear from you again, Devin. It's over between you and I. I'll get back with my ex before I think about giving you another chance." I stood up abruptly, almost causing him to lose his balance. I walked over to my pile of dirty clothes by the door and picked them up. With my free hand, I unlocked and cracked the door open for him.

"Please leave my key on the coffee table and excuse yourself." He stood up and eyed me disappointedly.

"I can't do that baby, we built too much for me to let you throw away what we have." I shook my head no, as he approached me. He walked back towards the couch and went into his Gucci backpack that he loved carrying around like it was his purse. He pulled out my paperwork that looked like a thick packet and tossed it onto the glass coffee table.

"That's a deal baby, a deal for one million dollars. You can't get this deal if you just leave me. The CEO of Capital Records wants to fuck with you. I told you I was gon' get you far, I just needed time." I licked my lips and dropped my clothes and walked all the way back into the living room space.

"So why now, Devin? Why when you do me wrong and cheat on me, you pull out some fucking papers expecting me to jump for joy. Like I'm your fucking slave! I've watched you skip me multiple times and get plenty of people deals. You never wanted me to fucking shine, now that I'm done with you, your producing papers that I have been waiting on from you for years? Fuck that and fuck you! Ain't no telling how long you have had those papers. Please get out of my home before I call the police on you." I spat with my heart beating fast inside my chest.

"I'll blackball you, Era. You will never step a foot in the industry fucking with me. Don't make this shit hard." He spoke in a chill tone. I had to step back and laugh a little. The real him was being exposed.

"Well, I guess you better get ya black book out and start blackballing me." I walked away and picked my clothes back up. Making my way into my bedroom, I slammed and locked the door. Placing my clothes in the dirty clothes hamper, I sat at the edge of my bed holding my breath. I was waiting for Devin to let himself out of my house so I could let my raw emotions flow freely.

I almost caught myself growing weak, a part of me wanted to work it out just for the sake of that million-dollar contract. My momma always told me that I had a true gift and to never sell myself short. This was the proof of that. Devin had lots of connections in the industry, and I believed him to the fullest when he said that he would blackball me.

That's what hurt the most. The fact of him wanting to hurt me when I wasn't the one in the wrong. He flipped the script fast, soon as he realized that I was standing my ground. I heard my front door slam and glass shattering on my tile floor. Going into the living room, I was pleased that he left my spare key. The contract was gone, and he slammed the door so hard that the big picture frame of me and him on vacation fell and shattered.

I was back to being alone and my small apartment with nothing but loud thoughts roaming through my head. I knew I made the right decision and should be very proud of myself, but it hurt like hell. Not only did I break up with the man I loved, but he walked out with an opportunity that would be hard for me to come across again.

I sat on the couch in silence for a while until I heard knocking at my door again. Sighing hard preparing myself to tell Devin to go the fuck away, I opened the door, and my mom was standing there all frowned up with her small baby gun in her hand. I smiled weakly and stepped to the side letting her in. Soon as she put her purse and gun down, I fell right into her arms and cried myself to sleep in her arms in my living room. This just couldn't be life.

PRAYLAH

I wanted to feel good because, after weeks of working hard and balancing being a mom of my own kid and Jarei's son, I finally had some freedom. Heaven was at my parent's house for the entire week, and I hadn't heard from Nyla or Jarei. Speaking of Jarei, he came and went as he pleased, which was super confusing to me. It's been two weeks since he has been home and the last time that I actually saw him he was grabbing lots of clothes saying how he had to make an important play out of town.

I was shocked that he even left me with a thousand dollars, which was a plus for me. I put that money to the side for when it came time to having to pay our bills. I wanted to ask him why he had to be gone for so long, but I wouldn't dare pry into his business and set him off on a rampage.

I needed the space from him mentally and to be able to get the rest that I needed. I didn't get any breaks so whenever my parents called me asking for Heaven, I jumped on that immediately. Cooking and cleaning plus giving Heaven the attention and love she needed was very important to me.

Things back at the restaurant had picked up and I found

myself working more doubles. I had two days off and today would be my first day back at work. I would be posing as manager since Era was going through a hard break up. I felt super bad for my best friend because she would literally give you the clothes off her back to make sure the people she loved were good.

I also admired her strength and her being able to walk away from a man not valuing her for the good woman that she was. Now all I had to do was find my own strength and get myself out of my own toxic situation. I dressed in some slacks and a white button-down shirt today, finding my bowtie and name tag, I put both on and headed straight for the bus stop with jitters filling my stomach.

For the past two weeks, the handsome intimidating man that I spilled a drink on had been coming by the restaurant ordering the same thing almost every time he came in. He also sat in the same spot and would often mumble things to himself. I caught him plenty of times watching me like he was studying for a test. Every now and then he'd scan and watch the rest of the restaurant like he was waiting for something to go wrong.

Maybe I was overthinking things or bugged out by our first encounter. He made me nervous, and I made it a point not to serve as his waiter. The wild look in his eyes whenever my eyes landed on him sent chills up and down my spine and heated my entire insides.

I used to think Jarei was intimidating and unhinged, one look at this stranger and it's like he had trouble written in cursive all over his nice physic. An unfamiliar jolt of electricity went through me each time he offered me that crazed pensive stare. Nothing about him gave, nice or gentle and easy going. He was a beast and his unique dangerous look added to just that.

His build was massive, like a giant. Even his beard that was oiled and shiny looked tantalizing. He looked unapproachable, which was the main reason I had so many jitters the day he looked up and stared deep into my soul. I could no longer feel the glass that day as it slipped from my hand, I felt him, all of him staring deep into me. It was as if I could feel him, like he summoned my entire being.

I probably sounded crazy as hell right now, but it was hard to explain the kind of pull this man had on me from the very first encounter.

I made it to work thirty minutes early, since I was posing as manager I got right to work and didn't waste any time. I always wanted to show and prove my work ethics because I needed this job desperately. I needed any and everything that I could get, I was saving to be able to buy me and Heaven a car. I wanted to find the same strength that Era had, I was living with a man that didn't give a damn about me anymore.

I was holding on for the love that I still held for him, even the respect. I had lots of respect and maintained my loyalty for Jarei, regardless of all the foul things he had done to me in front of my face and behind my back. I wanted Heaven to have both of her parents just like I did when I grew up. My parents were the perfect representation of love and what it was supposed to look like.

Thinking about Jarei and our failed relationship took me to a dark place and made me feel super emotional. Feeling like I was wasting nothing but time from never giving up on him had me believing that I was nothing more but a weak bitch to him. The spark was long gone and what I needed to do was accept my reality.

I went to the back office that Era handled business at, in the back of the restaurant and gathered the strength and courage to call Jarei.

"Yea, Pray? Getting to the money right now." He sounded agitated by me interrupting him, but he always sounded that way whenever I did reach out or talk to him in person.

"We need to talk tonight, it's really important," I spoke clearly so he could know that it was serious.

"We can speak over the phone; I didn't plan on coming home tonight." Rolling my eyes, I got mad at the tears already gathering in the sockets of my eyes. The worse feeling was being at work trying to focus when you had your significant other heavy on your mind. I couldn't understand for the life of me why Jarei even wanted to be with me when he acted like everything about me disgusted him.

"If you really want this thing between us, you will be home tonight. I can't keep going on like this." I hung up in his face and quickly texted him the time to be expecting me home. After the text said, *delivered*, I blocked his number so he couldn't further mess up my day. Jarei liked to talk bad to me through text making me feel bad. I wanted to desperately make this shit work with us because of the love that I refused to let go. I thought about all the years and time I put into this, all the sacrifices and didn't want it all to go to waste.

Feeling good about myself, I got busy and helped to my full ability around the restaurant. I could feel the bottom of my feet throbbing and took a break. When I got back from break, I stepped into the front of the restaurant and noticed the sun was going down. We didn't close super late on weekdays so today would be an early day which meant I would be closing and cleaning the kitchen then locking up the restaurant.

My eyes scanned the entire restaurant, and they landed on the stranger who sat with a table full of thugs. They talked and laughed and threw back shots. Me and the stranger's wild eyes connected, and I quickly diverted my attention. Usually,

I caught him looking at me, but today he caught me looking at him. My mouth went dry, and like a Nat being attracted to fruit, I couldn't stop my eyes from looking up again and meeting his.

This time, he offered a smile with just his eyes, it didn't reach his lips. With his elbows resting on the table, he motioned for me to come here with his index finger. I shook my head no and stopped when I realized I was telling a good-paying customer no. I frantically walked to the back of the restaurant and found a waiter by the name of Holly.

I sent her to go see what it was he wanted and busied myself with something other than spying on a total stranger that actually creeped me the fuck out. His arms appeared the size of Hulk Smash arms, all the tattoos covering his nutmeg skin tone didn't take away from his blemish-free smooth skin. The black V-neck shirt hugged him kind of tight exposing all the ripples he had.

He looked to be uninterested in what his boys were talking about like his mind was on other things until those demanding gray orbs landed on me. Shaking my head by how caught up I was over him, I glanced at the time, and it was nearing closing time.

By the time I closed everything and made sure the staff had cleaned up the eating area, I went to the office to put the money up into the wall safe. Rolling my sleeves up and putting my phone on the R&B pandora station. I sat my phone down and prepared myself to tighten up an already clean kitchen area then checked the rest of the place out to make sure it was perfect for opening in the morning.

"Pray-"

Startled, scared, and confused I turned around to face the most unique-looking man whom I accidentally spilled water on. In my mind I thought and knew he wasn't supposed to be back here and that he crossed the line. He had a wild crazed look in his gray eyes, licking his thick full lips, and moving in closer to me as he chanted my name like a fucking maniac.

"Praylah, Praylah. I feel like you really fucked up." Looking him in his eyes seemed to be too much, the intensity and the way he didn't blink while maintaining eye contact had me shaken. His black dreads hung loosely past his shoulders; they looked like he just had received a fresh retwist.

I blinked once, and when I opened my eyes, he was so close to me that I could smell Wrigley's Five peppermint gum on his breath.

"Soon, you will end up being a prey of mine, Praylah." I couldn't even control myself. That stupid trembling shit I did when I was nervous started to happen. My bottom lip started shaking like it was below zero degrees in the kitchen. Holding onto the mop to keep me grounded, I finally found my voice.

"I'm sorry, sir the restaurant is closed and ummm… you can't be back here." Offering me a deranged smirk he grabbed the bottom of my chin and forced me to look right back into his chanting eyes.

"You nervous, but you crazy as fuck like me." His low rumble laugh hit my core. "I think you a lil ditzy as fuck too. I just told you, that I'm making you my prey and you say some other shit that I don't give a fuck about." Stepping back from his closeness didn't make a difference because his thick thumb and index finger held on tighter to my chin.

"I'll call the police." Ugh what the fuck was I thinking. "I'm sorry, I don't want any problems but you're making me uncomfortable sir."

"You're scared?" I nodded my head yes, hoping that he would get the picture.

"No sir, I'm petrified."

"You like being tied up, don't you? Shackles at your ankles with those thick thighs spread wide and all that freaky shit." He bit into his bottom lip and kept it in place. Moving his hand from my chin, his rough fingertips traced over the makeup that I had piled on top of my birthmark.

"I don't sir." I spoke above a whisper.

"You keep calling me sir, making my dick hard as fuck. I'm trying to approach you on some grown man shit. I waited until the restaurant closed to get yo fuckin' number. Now you keep carrying on with all this sir, sir, sir. It's like you ready for me to take you home and tie you the fuck up." He smirked and stepped closer; I stepped back. A look of frustration crossed his crazy-looking eyes. He huffed releasing a harsh breath and grabbed me by the waist pulling me close.

"Ahhhh!" I screamed and threw my hands up, only for him to catch my wrist and squeeze tight.

"I like that scary, timid shit. It's how a prey supposed to feel when its predator is after it. Stop all that fucking screaming, I don't take pussy, its given to me." He released me with a slight push.

"Give me yo number, so I can talk to you outside of my place of business and I want to see you without all this clown shit covering your face." He looked at his fingertips then back up at me accusingly. I felt embarrassed because I probably over did it with the makeup this morning. I was in a rush and really didn't blend properly so I was sure a lot of my cheap foundation was on his fingers.

I was more stuck on him claiming that this was his business. He was the owner so that meant he was responsible for signing my checks. I licked my lips and fell into my thoughts forgetting that he was standing right in front of me. I was trying to choose my words wisely because I didn't need my boss feeling compelled to fire me. Why the hell did Era not tell me this? Now it made sense why he was here so much.

He looked dangerous and very deadly, I took one glance at his massive hands and could tell they were made for destruction.

"You own Beastly Cravings?" I wanted to be sure as I stood in disbelief. He probably came just to spy and make sure people were running his five-star establishment like we were supposed to. He shrugged and looked at his fingertips then back up to my face like what I had said wasn't something to be excited about.

"Yea, it's one of my many franchises. Don't tell anybody around this bitch what you just learned tonight though? You hear me?" I quickly nodded my head as he gave me a mischievous smirk.

"So, give me your number, so we can be out this bitch. It's late as fuck and since you don't have a car, I'll drop you off at home."

"How do you know that I don't have a car?" I placed my hand on my hip not feeling scared like that anymore. Sure, it was evident with his approach and the way his eyes seemed to zone out every couple of seconds like he was conflicted about something showed that he was crazy. His crazy ass took a liking to me so now was my turn to not appear like some weak bitch in front of him. I think he took note of the change I was taking, and he chuckled lowly, his voice dropping low and a guttural tone.

"My Maserati is the only fuckin' car out in the parking lot. You ain't got no car, now all of a sudden you bold but still ditzy as fuck. I don't really want to ask you for your number again, this shit is crazy." He mumbled the last part, rubbing his hands through his beard.

"I have a fiancé and a one-year-old daughter, to respect my

man and myself I will have to pass on the ride home and giving you my number." I swallowed down hard and made small eye contact with him as I took in the kitchen. It looked clean enough, so I guess it was time for me to get going. I needed to get far away from this man, I wouldn't dare disrespect myself or Jarei for that matter no matter how bad our relationship was.

I was determined to get my relationship back on track and tonight was the night that I planned on laying things out in the open for Jarei and I. I was tired of always holding back and being so timid and scared to speak my mind. If I could face a handsome and big scary man like the one and front of me than I could do the same with my own man.

"We don't give a fuck." Finally, he blinked twice like he had realized that he spoke as if it was two of him present. Clearing his throat and leaning against the metal countertop, he shook his head like he was battling with something other than me denying him of my time and attention. The caring side of me wanted to know what was wrong.

"I'm fucked in the head; whole mental be off. My apologies if I'm coming off like a creep and shit. I just think beyond all that shit that you got on your face, you beautiful as fuck. Like you, I don't know, I feel like I got to get to know you." It's like he did a quick three-sixty in front of me. Ignoring the him wanting to get to know me part, I decided to dig deep and ask him some questions.

"What do you mean when you say your mental is off?" I asked softly, not really knowing why I was deciding to be so bold and walk a little closer to him. It felt like I was walking towards danger.

"I'm fucked up in the head, I be hearing shit, well a voice. I already feel like I'm soulless, Ma. That voice sometimes sounds like the devil chanting in my ear. Like its constantly on go and want me to be crazier. I don't even know how to explain that shit. I guess I fed that voice for so many years, its apart of me." He shrugged his big shoulders then looked off momentarily.

"To be honest, I never expressed this shit to nobody. Something about you though that got me wanting to tell you my whole life. You wouldn't be able to handle that shit though, if I started from the very beginning, in seconds, you'd be running out the back door." He chuckled lowly and shook his head.

"Let me take you home, though. You don't need to be on the bus this late. I know I started off aggressive with you. For some reason that fucking voice in my head is in love with you and don't want to back down from having you." He had a need in his voice that made me want to fulfil whatever the need was. Reality was his problems weren't mine although I could see the emptiness and sadness evident all in his gray sexy orbs.

The logical side of me knew it would be wrong for me to even entertain and try to be close with this man. From what he said, he battled with some mental issues that he needed professional help with. A sane person would never say the things that he had just said. I felt like I connected with him in an instance due to my own mental problems that I couldn't seem to help at times but forced myself to for the sake of my daughter.

"I have bipolar disorder. Sometimes I go into deep depression, and I end up feeling and believing the fucked-up things that people tend to tell me about myself." I left out the fact that Jarei was the person that told me all of those mean things. "I, umm, take medicine. I like feeling pain just to snap me into reality and I know it's not something healthy, so I take medicine to boost my mood. When I want to feel happy and energized for my one-year-old."

I guess I felt open enough to tell him about my personal problems since he was telling me about his. I never met someone that battled with their mental, so it made me feel super comfortable.

"All yo nigga gotta do is fuck you hard and make it painfully good. There's your pain right there, Ma. Or does he do that for you?" He stood from leaning against the counter and neared me again. I trembled a little and tilted my head back to stare into his eyes. My goodness he was so tall and so close to me that I smelled whatever intoxicating fragrance he had on. His voice was so heavy and thick with a dash of smoothness to it.

Him speaking about sex, something that I wasn't getting at home seemed to heighten all of my senses. He was dominating and irresistible even, I needed to get away from him. I don't know why I opened up and admitted to my problems. He had a determined look to solve any problem that I told him.

"Michael." His thick voice seemed to caress my lady parts.

"Huh?" he rumbled a low sexy laugh.

"My name is Michael." He held his hand out and I slowly took it into mine. Something transpired between the both of us soon as my hand landed in his and I jolted a little, blinking rapidly, I took my hand out of his.

"Let me get you home, Praylah. I think we had a great introduction to each other, for now." He smiled and my heart sped up rapidly, his teeth were super white and perfectly aligned. This man was dangerous, trouble that I didn't need and the fucked-up part about it was I felt there was no escaping him because he was my boss.

PRAYLAH

The entire ride, it was hard for me to keep my eyes off of Michael. We pulled a couple of houses down from my house and he wiped his hand over his mouth then looked over at me with an intense look. My heart slammed against my ribs as he offered me a pensive questioning look.

"This not your house." He smirked and turned a little in his seat to look me over. I shifted uncomfortably but didn't want him to sense that I was lying.

"Umm, how do you know?" This man was really driving me crazy and didn't even know it.

"Umm..." he mocked me then smiled. "You love saying *umm* when you nervous, huh?" He reached over, I flinched, and a rough chuckle escaped his thick lips. He pulled a piece of my hair softly and released it letting it bounce back in place.

"I know exactly where you live, I already looked into that. I was just giving you the benefit of the doubt to lead me to the right house. I hope you don't think you having a man at home can deter me from anything, Pray." Licking his top row of perfect teeth. I reach down between my legs for my purse, my grasp is tight from all this anticipation of what he will surprise me with next.

"I wouldn't stalk you, unless you owed me some shit. I wouldn't hurt or fuck you without permission either, Praylah. To subdue a woman is all about control, I don't control you yet so I can't subdue you. It's just a little comical because I can smell you, literally." I didn't know what the hell he was even talking about, but it seemed like my body did.

"You're a submissive and sweet woman, a good girl. Whoever your man is, is lucky as fuck but his luck is running out fast. No woman that appears the way you appear, should be relying on public transportation. Your nails, hair and feet should be done and a constant glow from being dick down properly should shine as bright as the sun and fuckin' moon." Michael's deep accented voice slides across my skin like silk and wraps itself around me.

I was so speechless, the only thing that I could offer him was a soft sigh. Placing his car in drive, he didn't say anything else as he drove further down my street and stopped right in front of my house. Placing his car in park he looked over at me, as I swallowed down all nervousness. It felt like my breath was stuttering as he sucked me into his deep gaze. His eyes, I can't even explain it properly, but his eyes had a haunting chill to its beauty that held my gaze to his. It's hard to break and before I know it, his hands are somewhere they don't belong.

I'm so wrong for this and I feel shameful, but I can't find my voice to save my life. My stomach clenches, our attraction is sky high. His hands descended down my pants, past my stomach that's protecting my most prized possession. Not seeming to care, Michael smoothly but boldly pushes past the stranger boundary and slide his middle finger down my slit purposely bumping against my swollen clit.

Finally, being pushed back into reality, I grab his forearm to stop him, shaking my head no from being petrified at the mere feeling and sensations running through me. My body wouldn't stop trembling from the bold move he made. Surprisingly, he stopped and then removed his callous hand from between my thick thighs. Chuckling, he got out of the car and slammed the door shut. I watch him walk around to the passenger side and open up my door with the hand that he just had between my legs behind his back.

Once I step out the car, he brings that hidden hand around to the front of us and licks his moist finger. Grunting, then licking again, his gaze hit mine with a flicker of acknowledgment in his eyes.

"You gone be my sugar mommy, so fucking sweet, satisfying as fuck to taste. Keep that pussy in a safe place for me. I'll see you soon Praylah." He walked away leaving me standing there gasping for air. That was the weirdest encounter of my life, it left me forgetting that Jarei was home waiting for us to have this grand conversation that could get us back right with our relationship.

I turned away from Michael's car with a massive flood between my thighs. With each step I took, my pussy felt slippery like it wanted to fall right from being attached to me and chase right after Michael and jump on him for the deliverance he was offering.

Shaking my head and saying a silent prayer, I didn't turn around to look back at Michael's car. I could still hear the low rumble of his engine behind me. Reaching inside my purse, I fished for my keys and entered my house. Feeling relieved to get far away from my boss who had me still shaken up from our explosive encounter.

Taking off my shoes, I felt like I was missing something. My Heaven, I missed my baby already and it hadn't even been long since she had been away at my parent's house. I could smell the weed smell that lingered in my house and knew that Jarei was probably in our bedroom smoking it out, sitting at the edge of our bed waiting for me.

A random thought crossed my mind, and I was disappointed in myself that the thought was surrounding Michael. He gave me the option to tell him the truth about where I lived when he already knew all along. Had he looked deep into me, I was sure he was capable and had the money to do such things.

Turning the corner and opening my bedroom door, I walked right into Jarei's fist. My body hit the carpet with a loud thud and my head started throbbing hard. I couldn't even see straight the only thing I could think to do was shield my face and body to the best of my ability.

"Bitch!" He grabbed a handful of my already kinky curly hair and pulled it. I felt my hair ripping from my scalp. The pain was excruciating and so unbearable that I couldn't find my voice to scream or shout.

"Don't you ever in your fat funky miserable life call me on some demanding we talk type of shit!" Wham! Another closed fist hit that knocked my hands away from my mouth. Jarei was in a rage and couldn't be stopped. At least not by me, every time I opened my eyes, I saw silver and purple stars. Wham!

"I swear, I'm sick of you bitch! Always walking around this muthafucka sad and looking lost like you ain't got no fucking back bone! You bad luck for a nigga, got me out here hustling hard tryna make money, niggas ain't respecting who the fuck I am. Then I get a call from my fat ass girlfriend demanding I come home when I'm trying to make some fucking money! Bitch-" Wham! This time my front two teeth were knocked down my throat and I choked and gagged hard to bring them back up.

Panicking, I placed my finger deep into my mouth forcing myself to throw up. Once my bile rose and the throw up spilled from my mouth onto my carpet, I could feel myself breathing better. Jarei was a monster, and this was the furthest he ever went, I couldn't even bring myself to stare up at him.

"I don't know what I ever even saw in you, pathetic as fuck, keep gaining weight, miserable ass bitch. Only good thing you do is take care of my kids, so again and for the last time… let me remind you Praylah, you ain't going nowhere. Ain't no nigga gon' want your unstable crazy in the head ass. Barely clean yo ass and wonder why I won't touch you." He chuckled and I could hear him out of breath sitting down on the bed.

"I do wash my ass." I pitifully defended myself. I was disgusted at the sound of my voice. It sounded like I was now talking with a lisp with my swollen lips and missing teeth. At times, I would get so depressed with my bipolar disorder, feeling so down in the dumps that I would miss a shower or two. I would feel so fucked up and lost that I could only gather enough strength to take care of Heaven.

"I don't want this anymore." I cried out hard, hiccupping and coughing roughly. I almost gagged on my own spit. "I will take care of the kids, but I can't with you anymore Jarei. Your breaking-" I looked up at his balled-up face and broke down hard. Why did I love him so much?

"You're breaking me down Jarei, and I don't know why when I love you. I have never done you wrong, I try my best even through suffering. I try everything and you hate me, and I don't know why. I can't do this anymore, I don't want you, you're going to kill me Jarei." My eyes filled with so much liquid that I became blinded. My head hurt, my body and heart felt like it was being ripped into shreds.

"Shut the fuck up, weak ass bitch." He stood and walked out of the room. I knew he didn't leave the house because I heard the living room TV cut on. Jarei's problem was he liked to take his frustrations out on me. I never got involved in his street problems, I never asked him what was going on because I didn't care to know.

I barely took money from him or even asked him for any kind of money. Whatever money he gave to me when he was attempting to be nice, I never treated myself to something nice with it. I would just put it to the side for bills for when he came to me with excuses on why he couldn't help with our expensive ass rent.

He flexed a lot to his friends, making his boys believe he had it like that when he really didn't. The Benz he drove around in was glued to my name, his car note was seven hundred dollars, he made sure he paid that while I was stuck with the insurance. He picked this house for us to rent, claiming he didn't want to be in the hood for the chances of someone trying to rob us. Whatever Jarei wanted, I went right along with it with stress in the pits of my being, knowing if things took a turn, it would be on me.

My family was the kind of family that didn't believe in helping you out if you claimed to have a man. They felt like if you had a man then he should be providing so I never embarrassed myself and asked for a helping hand. I picked my battered ass right off the floor and dragged my feet to the bathroom scared to look at my reflection. I knew that this time, Jarei went too far, and the damage was horrible.

I also knew that I had to get away from him, with my mental state and the way I was feeling right now at this very moment was dangerous. Looking up at myself in the mirror, something inside of me snapped. My left jaw was swollen, my mouth swollen, rib cage aching. I didn't deserve this, none of this. All of this came from wanting a conversation with my man to better our relationship.

Jarei was hateful and downright evil, it could only get worse from here. I had a deep fear in the core of my soul. At night sometimes I'd dream of him killing me and leaving my daughter to fend for herself. This was a relationship beyond repair, I had to push my wants to the far end of my mind and focus on me and Heaven's needs. Right now, I needed to get away from him and get a better grip on my life. I had to put a successful plan in place, I needed to get to Era, she would help me come up with the perfect plan to escape Jarei.

DEBO

My knuckles tighten as I twist my wrist, just as this nigga's eyes widen in fear. I got a high off the satisfaction as my fist collided right into his chin. *Now kill this mutha fucca! Show that nigga standing next to you what's to come if he does some hoe shit!* I looked over at Sosa, he gave a look like he wasn't impressed, and neither was I. We both put hard beatings on niggas, the difference was, I could kill a pussy nigga with my bare hands.

I didn't know why that voice in my head wasn't really fuckin' with Sosa but the more it talked the more I fed it. Sosa was my nigga, but coming to me for a handout like I wasn't gon' hit him with a fee is probably what had that voice livid.

Having enough of using my fist, I pulled my blade out and that's when all the begging erupted from this soon to be dead niggas mouth.

"Die slow, should've never did business with them niggas from the south behind my fuckin' back." Stabbing his carotid artery, I knew he would die slowly. Something I liked especially for a nigga that showed disloyalty. It gave a person time to think and see how they fucked up with me, then they'd start wishing upon a star hoping that God gave them the ability to rewind time and try again.

"We sending his momma a severance packet?" I looked over at Honor, real down ass gutta bitch. I didn't consider many in the game to be my friend, but she was somebody that I spent lots of nights with. We used to grind until the sun went down until the middle of the night. I fucked with her heavy, her loyalty was as solid as mine. Which was why she was my General. I had a lot of shit legally going on that I had to constantly tend to. Honor stepped shit up and kept her foots on niggas neck, while maintaining her ears down to the concrete. Didn't shit get past her.

"Hell naw, tell slaughter gang to chop that nigga up in tiny pieces. His momma will have a missing person report out on him in about a week." She nodded her head, pulling out her burner phone, typing away she looked up when Sosa stupid ass said some dumb shit.

"You too pretty to be gay as fuck. I mean, I can see yo shape with them skinny jeans practically painted on." I shook my head hard at him. Honor looked like a straight-up nigga, as a female back when we were in high school, I saw her feminine once. She was bad as fuck. Over the years she turned into a pretty boy ass nigga. She was caramel, with high cheekbones and cat eyes. The bitches fucked with her heavily. Honor was real petite with a small bubble butt, she sagged her skinny jeans a little so you could see whatever designer briefs she rocked. I never could bring myself to look at her sexually because shit, she was a nigga in my eyes and that's how I respected her.

Today, instead of her long curly hair being braided down in straight backs. She had her curly hair all over her head and it stopped mid-back. Sosa's thirsty ass was trying his luck today, so if Honor decided to go nutty on this nigga, I wasn't gone hold her down or back from doing so.

"Shit, thanks but if I turn you on then that mean you gay as fuck nigga. Means you attracted to niggas or some shit." She took her cigarette from behind her ear and sparked it. I motioned for her to give me one and she tossed the pack my way.

"I'm attracted to pussy, and you got one. You ain't exempt." I chuckled and shook my head as Honor laughed a little too.

"Nigga you gay as fuck, fuck outta here. You a broke boy anyway, so even if I was into niggas, trust I'd never even look your way. That's the only reason you standing in this warehouse now, right? Tryna get a handout from the slaughter gang." She taunted with her hand on her hip. She wasn't on no sassy shit; Honor was ready to pull her gun and blast this nigga. Her draw down on any nigga walking was extremely fast.

"Bitch what the fuck you say?" Sosa attempted to walk past me, and I shoved him in the chest.

"Chill the fuck out nigga." I looked over at Honor and she already had her nine mili pointed in Sosa's direction.

"Put that shit away. Both of y'all my niggas so be easy. If y'all niggas emotional and can't take a fuckin' joke, then don't play around. I ain't no fuckin' babysitter so try that shit on somebody else's time. Honor, go get this nigga his bricks so we can all be out." I had a bad ass migraine; it probably was due to me not getting any sleep these past couple of days.

My mind was on too much, the center of my mind was mainly on Praylah. Her taste and scent, the nurturing vibe she gave off that made me feel like I could have peace with just her being near me.

When she spilled that water on me and I took her in, like really took her in, I just wanted to fuck. Getting a conversation out of her made me want more something I knew I wasn't ready for but wanted.

"Gave that nigga two bricks to start off with. If he don't move that in two weeks then we don't need to do no future business with them M.G.N niggas." I nodded my head because Honor was right. I told her shoot my boy Sosa three books, but she was smart giving that nigga two. Homie or no homie, I'd kill a nigga dead over one brick. The principal was just that, so I understood why she only gave that nigga two.

"Nigga was born a hustler like us, he gone be back in less than two weeks tops." I reassured her.

"I hope so, cause you know it ain't shit for me to put his broke ass in the dirt." I looked off at nothing in particular. This warehouse smelled like death. All we did was store shit then kill shit in this muthafucka.

"You seem like you been having shit on ya mind. What's good Debo?" Honor pulled two cigarettes out just as some of my men started walking in to take the body, I just caught to the back room that we called slaughterhouse. I didn't know why niggas constantly thought they could get away with just small things and think they didn't have to face consequences. Niggas got killed like it was going out of style. You'd think a nigga would tighten up and get smart. Make ya money, take care of ya family and keep some loyalty. Sticking to the G code was law, I didn't see shit no other way.

"Met the love of my life." There wasn't no other way to put it. Praylah had my mind on her too damn much. I wanted to pull up to her house, knock on her door then drag her ass back to my place then keep her there forever. That wasn't some logical shit, she was too timid, nothing like the bitches I was used to sticking. With Praylah, she had issues. Some that she revealed, her light was dim as fuck, and she needed a nigga like me to relight her shit.

I ran both hands over my full face and sighed. I didn't even know how I could fit a woman like Praylah in my everyday life, but I needed to figure out a way. She was mysterious, soft spoken and had an innocence in her eyes when she gave me her full attention. I wanted her and was determined to get her. Even with the background check that I did, I didn't bother looking into who her nigga was.

Truth was whoever he was didn't matter unless he tried to matter. I looked at whoever he was as keeping her company until I found out the best approach. After I got my shit straight and had the perfect way to get up with her then the rest was going to be history. If that nigga even dared to try bucking up, then I was gone become the worse nightmare he ever had in reality.

"Damn Debo, you really got it bad as fuck!" Honor laughed at me, I couldn't help but shake my head and chuckle lowly. I zoned out just thinking about Praylah thick sugar sweet ass.

"I gotta get her, but the cold part is… I don't know how." That was the truth, I never put no type of work in to get or knock a female. They always came to me, and I decided which ones were worthy enough.

"Ask for a date, don't be too intimidating and hardcore so she can feel welcomed to going out with you."

"She got a nigga, and her loyalty is concrete. Dropped her off at home and his car was home. I wanted to kick her door down and beat his ass for making his woman catch the bus at night while he at home." I gritted, popping my knuckles.

"Shit, that should tell you something bout her." Honor mumbled and I immediately looked up at her with a glare.

"Don't get crazy nigga, I'm just saying. Women that let

niggas dog them got issues and low self-esteem problems." She shrugged, taking a hit of her cigarette. I took my lighter out and sparked mine.

"She might be a lil like that, she got a one-year-old. She probably feels like she ain't got no other choice but to stick with the nigga." Females loved their baby daddies; they allowed them to get away with foul shit hoping to keep their little fake fucked up family together.

"How the fuck you meet her anyway?" I took a drag from my Newport and smiled crookedly.

"She works at Beastly Cravings."

"I thought you don't fuck with the help." She giggled as we started walking towards the back door where our cars were parked.

"I don't but had to make an exception."

She shook her head and flicked her cigarette across the parking lot.

"Thissss nigga. I can't wait to meet her man."

"Yeap, my lil suga momma." I mumbled that last part, Honor wasn't supposed to hear that, but she did and she cracked jokes hard on me.

"So, she old?" She leaned up against her Denali. I never understood how and why her short ass had such a massive damn car. She drove crazy as hell and half the time she ran up on sidewalks trying to turn corners.

"Hell naw, I just call her that for personal reasons." I smirked and hit the locks to my car. Chunking up slaughter gang, we said our goodbyes and I decided to head to my main house to see what was up with Lakendra. She had been calling me all day for the last past couple of days and I was getting tired of it. I decided to let her have the fucking house. I didn't want to because I had that shit built from the ground up, it was one of my first pieces of property, so I took pride in it.

All the shit I put her through, she deserved that and more, so I was willing to sacrifice and turn the house over to her. I wanted to put Lakendra in the past, but my guiltiness didn't make that shit quite easy.

I sat in my car for a moment contemplating my next move. My phone vibrated and I saw that it was my dad calling. Pressing ignore had me feeling guilty as fuck, soon my father was gone force his way around and whenever he did that, it became ugly. Trying to get my mind off of possible consequences that I was sure to face by going toe to toe with my dad, I went to my contacts and clicked on the name stored in as Suga Momma. Hearing the phone ring had me smiling. I was ready to fuck her mind up for the day then go about my own day.

"Hello?" I frowned at the way she was now talking, like she was tongue tied or some shit.

"I'm trying to figure you out, get to know you. Right now, I'm just assuming Love. I think you need attention, to feel secure and safe. You need the kind of love and reassurance that can only come from a nigga like me. Give your daughter a stepdad that makes her momma feel like a queen and her a princess." I bit my bottom lip to keep from laughing at myself. I sounded like a straight-up simp and if Honor or any of my niggas was around to hear me speak this way, they'd clown me hard as fuck.

"Michael?" Her soft voice was fucking my head up. I wanted to go right to her at this moment but knew I wasn't ready for her yet.

"Don't play that ditzy shit with me, Pray. You been fuckin' that nigga that you call ya man?" I gripped the phone tightly; I didn't have the right by then again, I did. Usually when I gave someone a direct order, they didn't have a choice in the matter.

"No, he umm hur- we having problems. I'm battling with my mind right now trying to stay sane and positive for my baby." I could hear the sadness in her voice, and I automatically wanted to make it better for her.

"When can I see you? Without all the makeup? You can even bring baby girl, I can take y'all out to eat."

"That's not a good idea. I don't know you, so I wouldn't bring my daughter around you. Plus, that would be disrespectful to her father, don't you think?" I could hear her clearly now; she was talking with a fucking lisp.

"I respect that and you even more, never bring a stranger around your kids when you ain't filled the stranger danger out yet." We both shared a laugh together.

"Why the fuck you sound like you missing teeth and shit." I leaned my head back against the headrest and watched my slaughter boys walk out of the warehouse with duffel bags. They took care of the body that fast; my niggas were the best at what they did.

"I ummm..." That umm shit irritated the fuck out of me. I noticed she did that shit when she was nervous about some shit. "Had an accident and my two front teeth were knocked out." Hanging the phone up in her face, I called Era while starting my car.

"Yes, Mr. Brownston?" Era sounded all perky, but my mind was on murder.

"Praylah... she at work?" I got right to the point skirting out the parking lot.

"No, she didn't come in, she hurt herself doing something at home. I gave her a couple of days off." Hanging up in her face, I jumped on the freeway just as my annoying ass sister was calling me.

"Fuck you want, Tea?" I had tunnel vision trying to maneuver through traffic to make it to Praylah.

"You big dick head! Daddy has been calling your nutty stupid ass, and you been dodging all of us! That's not how you treat people that care about you dummy! Kachella and Keem got married last week where the fuck were you for your sister! She cried because of you, and you still haven't reached the fuck out! It's been over a month!"

"I've been busy." I nonchalantly responded but instantly felt like shit. I didn't mean to miss Kachella's wedding. Kachella was spoiled and sometimes I forgot she was even a triplet to my brothers. I would cut a big check just to get back in my little sister's good graces and make this shit up.

"I swear Michael; sometimes you act like you don't have a family. We can see it clearly that you're battling something. It hurt me that you act like you can't even come to me and if not me at least daddy." Her voice softened, which was rare as fuck. Mattea was as heartless as I was. She just started having a heart for things when she got married and had kids of her own.

"I gotta sort my shit out, once I do, I'll be open to talk." I loved the fuck out of my family, but they made me feel incapable of standing on my own shit as a man. I had a problem with accepting and receiving help from anyone. Our father was very controlling when it came to our lives. Not wanting to see us fail or walk in the light that he had made him paranoid. He constantly rode us hard and stayed all in our mix. When I got old enough to make my own money I did just that.

I wasn't about to let our dad control me with money, so I had my own whenever he decided to cut my running faucet off for not listening to whatever it was that he wanted us to do.

"Too late for that dick head! Daddy will be at your house later with Momma. I'll be right there cheering him on when he beats your ass." She beat me at what I did best and that was hanging right up in my face. Since they knew that I would be at my other house because I didn't like being in the same house as Lakendra, I decided to switch shit up tonight and go to my main house where Lakendra was just so I could dodge my family drama.

I got to Praylah house in thirty minutes, knocking at her door like I was twelve. I waited but I didn't have the patience to just stand here and wait any longer. Shaking my head for what I was getting ready to do, I prepared to knock her door down. I stopped when I heard her locks clicking, indicating that she was aware that someone was at the door. Slowly opening the door with shades covering her eyes and a mask covering her eyes, she kept the door cracked with just her face sticking out.

"Umm, Michael?" She nervously moved her head, angling it to look around me like she was shook.

"You can't be here." Her tone was hasty like she wanted me to leave. I could feel my jaw clenching tightly. I calmed myself but still I felt myself ready to explode. Cracking my neck, I started out speaking slowly.

"You ain't had no accident Ma, step to the side let me in so I can look at you." I tried to talk as comforting as possible. Lowkey, I didn't really want to see what she was hiding. If it was severe, it would probably send me in a rage that I didn't possibly need.

I could feel her vibes of pain, that shit radiated through me making my stomach hurt. *Kill! Kill! Kill!* that voice in my head was raging making it hard for me to concentrate. I watched her shoulders go down in defeat. She opened her door and stepped all the way to the side.

Allowing me in her space, I looked around slowly. From what I could see she had been shacking in her living room. The balled-up tissues thrown about on her couch and floor had indicated that she was heartbroken and stuck in depression. Her blackout curtains had the place dim, and a stench crossed my nose causing me to turn and look over at her.

"When the last time you washed your ass, Praylah." I didn't want to hurt her feelings; I didn't know how to even ask her the question nicely. My whole life I had been blunt, but something about her made me want to word things in a way that didn't come through as mean. She was as fragile as glass, and I didn't want to crack and possibly shatter her when she was already damaged and hurt.

Praylah had on dingy sweatpants and a worn-out-looking spaghetti strap white shirt. The stains on her shirt made me believe that she had been blowing her nose on her shirt, just not giving a fuck because she thought she was all alone. Damn, I was seeing her in one of her elements that probably required her to take whatever medication that could help her boost the way she was feeling up. Maybe I could make it better on my own, I didn't really know what the fuck I should be doing at this very moment.

"I don't know when I showered, I don't care." She shrugged and flopped down on the couch. "I don't even want company Michael. I just want to be alone right now. My body hurts and my mind is weak right now." She sighed through the mask.

"That's too bad, I'm here to help you Pray. Take that mask and those glasses off so I can help you."

"I don't want help; I want to feel how I feel right now. I don't even know why you seem to be interested in me. I'm a dirty ass bitch, I'm always depressed, and whenever I feel like I ain't worth shit I treat myself like shit and I don't bathe.

I don't have the energy to even clean my own ass. I let people walk all over me cause I don't have the strength to even challenge a person good enough, that's why you in my house." She chuckled dryly. "A total fuckin' stranger, in my house. Well, my boss in my house, seeing the real me. You should just leave before I disgust you. I'm not those picture-perfect bitches that you're used to. I get yeast infections if I eat the wrong foods, my panties ain't always clean looking. My own man won't fucking touch me and haven't touched me in months. Maybe close to a year. I ain't shit, Michael. You too perfect, for a woman like me." She gasped then swallowed down hard. Rocking back and forth holding herself like she didn't want to lose whatever grip of sanity that she had left she looked away from me.

I didn't know what to do, I felt like searching for whatever love I had inside of me and pouring it all into her. The confidence I had and whatever other good things that I had locked away in the depth of my soul, I wanted to give it all to Praylah. She shouldn't even feel the way that she was feeling.

The nigga that she was with knew that Praylah had a problem. Pussy nigga played on that shit, instead of elevating and helping her through her storm.

I walked away from her and went searching for her bathroom. First step was finding whatever medicine it was that she took and trying to give it to her. This shit had me feeling like this was some type of deja vu, my mom used to have to tend to my father just like this giving him his meds when he was on edge. I found her bathroom and decided to start her up a shower.

Going through her bathroom drawers I found her medicine. Walking out of her bathroom I walked back to the living room and stood still. Praylah's glasses and mask were off, and I got an instant headache as memories came speeding through my brain. Her eyes were swollen and underneath her left eye was blue, red and purple. Her lips were puffy as hell like someone suctioned the fuck out of them.

I felt nauseous because it felt like my past was right in front of my face. *That bitch fucked your enemy! Don't go soft and act like we were in the wrong!*

"We were in the wrong!" I mumbled lowly. *No, we weren't! Help Praylah and stop feeling guilty! Fuck Lakendra! This isn't about her!*

"I dogged her though! Dogged her bad, she had every right to fucking cheat!" I started pacing, I needed to feel justified right now. Anger was soaring through me, I needed a cigarette, something to take the edge off. Praylah looked up at me with bewilderment as if she was confused about what I was talking about.

Putting her medication down on the table, I turned to walk away and out of her house. Seeing her fucked up was fucking me and my mental up. *She fucked an enemy, so I beat her ass!*

"I gotta get some help." I placed my hand on the doorknob and reached for the door.

"Michael?" I froze and that voice in my head stopped raging.

"I need you right now." Her voice was weak, my heart slowed down and I turned to face her, still feeling on edge. I couldn't leave her even if I wanted to. She needed me, and I was starting to believe that I needed her.

DEBO

"I don't know if he's going to pop up. I don't want to cause you any problems." We stood inside Praylah's small bathroom. She still hadn't admitted to her nigga doing her dirty, but she didn't have to, I already knew the deal. That nigga beat her cold and she stood in front of me terrified as fuck.

"If that nigga walk through that door, you shouldn't fear for me. You should fear for him." I didn't even want to scare her by going into detail. I had already made it my business to find her baby daddy and dead him.

"I love him." I tugged at her shirt, and she caught the bottom of it. Seeing the reluctance in her eyes, I eyed her hard. Her cheeks were flushed red. I didn't give a damn about how hard or how much she loved that nigga. Soon, that shit would go away.

"Praylah, let me help you sugar mommy." I playfully smirked at her. She agreed back in the living room to take her medicine and asked me did I have some form of medication. I knew she asked that shit because of me randomly talking to myself. I was determined to beat my shit; I didn't feel like nothing was really wrong with me to be taking crazy pills.

"You're gonna be disgusted if you see me naked." She looked away and I grabbed her chin and made her eyes connect with mine.

"Nah, I like all yo thickness. That shit sexy as fuck. What's gon' disgust me is all this thickness being funky. I'm trying to bathe you from head to toe then take you up out of here for the rest of the day. Can I do that?" She blushed and slowly nodded her head. Happy that she didn't bother asking me any other questions, I undressed and left her clothes right in the middle of the bathroom floor.

She turned and I bit down on my bottom lip. Praylah's body was sexy as hell. Her giving me that round curvy ass to watch as she got into the shower had me removing my gun slowly from waist and sitting it down on the counter. I stripped down and got in right behind her, I needed to be hands on with her. Start giving her that confidence that she needed, she was a bad as fuck and I hated that she didn't see it in herself.

Stepping in behind her, I couldn't stop my dick from rising. Her red hair had darkened from the water pouring over her head. She stiffened in front of me, she felt my dick as I turned her around to face me.

"You so fuckin' pure, beautiful as hell. I need you to see that." I cupped her round face and kissed her slowly. Watching her wince and close her eyes as my tongue entered her awaiting my mouth, tears started seeping out the corners of her eyes. Placing my hands on her shoulders, I began massaging her shoulder blades moving my hands up to her neck then back out until I'm gripping her shoulders. Picking up a pink washcloth, I laid her head on my chest and reached for her Dove soap. Lathering the towel until it was soapy, I started at her neck and scrubbed her back.

I could feel her trembling in my arms as I moved the towel between her ass cheeks. This was a whole lot of ass, so I wasn't cleaning between her cheeks on some soft shit. I was really getting up in there, making sure she was getting cleaned properly.

I never bathed a woman a day in my life, this was some new shit. It made me feel good tending to her in this intimate way. I wanted to fuck all the love she had for her pussy ass baby daddy out of her. Rinsing the towel out, I grabbed her sponge loaf and worked my way around her body like I was already well acquainted with it.

Hearing her sigh and moan from my hands touching all over her had me ready to pin her ass against her shower walls and take her ass down. Self-control was a bitch right now, that shit was slipping through my fingertips.

I made her rinse all the soap off, then went in again bathing her while gripping and grabbing her wet body.

"You want to get away from that nigga?" She looked at me desperately and nodded her head yes.

"Good, I got a spot close by Beastly Cravings. I don't want shit from you in return. You can even pay me rent. It's nothing fancy, it's clean and safe for you and your daughter. I won't even pop up acting like you owe me something. I just want to help you to move forward and heal."

Only thing I truly wanted in return when she got over this bitch ass niggas of hers was her heart and soul. Little did she know she already had my shit in her soft delicate hands. Just like that, I already decided that she was mine.

"That will work, I'm really done this time. I don't like how I feel this go round. The way he looked at me and talked, his hands…" she shivered and trembled even though the water was scorching hot.

"Don't even speak on it, I'm gon' see about him real soon." I looked off trying to remain calm.

"Matter fact, we don't got to discuss nothing right now. I just want you in a better headspace. I don't ever want to hear you talk about yourself like you did in the living room."

"Okay." Was all she said as my eyes left hers and scanned the rest of her slippery wet luscious body.

"I got a car you can use too." I offered already knowing she was gone try to decline. I planned on giving her Kachella's twenty-nineteen BMW. It was all pink, I bought it for her two birthdays ago. Now that shit sat in the garage collecting dust.

"I'll have it ready for you in a couple of days. Until then, I'll pick you up and take you to work." I wasn't trying to strip her of her independence, I probably was creeping her out enough by being so generous.

"Thank you, Michael. I will repay you; I promise I will." I hated how much her eyes got watery.

"Repay me by bossing up on anybody that ever doubted you sugar mommy. Repay me by loving you first, seeing and knowing that you sexy as fuck. Man, you got my head all fucked up. I want you so bad but I'm gon' wait. When I finally get you, Praylah… I ain't never letting you go. Our shit gone be explosive as fuck." She blushed and smiled weakly at me, I laid off her with words and helped her out the shower.

Entering her bedroom, I was still dripping all over her carpet. She stayed in the bathroom saying she had to put leave in conditioner in her hair or else it would have been too nappy looking. I told her to brush her hair in a ponytail. I wanted to see her full face with all her wild curls covering most of her face.

Entering her bedroom, I went to her closet where she said she kept extra dry off towels. Drying myself, I took a seat at the edge of her bed and waited for her to come out of the bathroom.

"I'm really grateful for you, Michael… I ummm… I don't want to depend on anyone for my happiness, I want to be able to make myself happy and have confidence. I hate you had to see me like that." She looked down at her feet. I stood and walked over to her, loving the fruity smell that came from her hair.

Even with swollen lips and bruises on her face, her beautiful, warm, vanilla skin tone still shined. Her hair was slick as hell going into a ponytail with the rest of her hair in a curly puff ball. Her hair wasn't bright red but a soft light fading red. She had high cheek bones that complimented her round sexy face.

"Preserve your dignity in tough times, Pray." I said in a low tone as I looked down at her short frame. Pulling her close by the small of her back, my hands slide down to squeeze her ass. Her delicate hands press up against my chest. I could feel when Praylah was nervous by the rise and fall of her chest.

"We don't even know each other good." She whimpered out as I bowed my head and kissed along her shoulder blades. Making her towel drop, we were now flesh to flesh.

"We know enough, we will know more along the way. Taking shit slow, I got a lot of shit that comes with me. I just know that I want you and nothing not even our mental states of minds will get in the way of that."

Cupping her face in my hands, I kissed her long and deep to reassure her how serious I was.

I can't help myself now, I got to feel her, she needs to feel me. We both need this shit. Walking her towards her full-size bed, I make her lay down. I watch those sad watery eyes, gnawing at her lips and gasping, her cheeks are flushed as fuck.

"What if he comes here, and see-"

"I'll kill him and continue to eat this pussy up." Feeling like I'm in a daze tuning out her worries, I focus on her wet slit that's seeping for me. I couldn't take this shit far with her, if I did it would scare the living shit out of her.

My sex drive was something out of this world, once my hunger soared, there was no stopping. Right now, I just wanted to make her feel good, help her release all of her frustrations. Lowering my face between her thighs and taking a deep sniff, I circle her clit softly and tease it until it swelled. Pushing just one finger deep inside of her, I latch onto her clit and suck slowly then lick hard until I feel her pussy gush then contract on my finger, locking my index finger with a death grip.

Sweet ass pussy, I grunt and try to put my entire face in her soppy center. Sliding my hands underneath her ass, I gave myself a better angle to devour every inch of her.

"Ohhhh, Michael." She gasped then sat up on her elbows to get a better view of me between her thighs. I looked up into her eyes, released her clit then kissed the fupa that was hovering above her mound.

"Daddy, call me daddy when I'm pleasing you baby." I latch back onto her clit with more force, her fingers twist into my nappy ass dreads, as she pulled my shit, I flatten my tongue and slide my tongue all around her sensitive bud.

"Oh, daddy! I'm-" she cut her own self off. Crying out to God, her hips buck against my face. Leaving her clit to throb, I suck all her juices into my mouth, I don't plan on stopping until she goes limp as fuck. Giving her a break, I kiss my way up until my wet lips are against her soft one and kiss her slowly, loving the sound of her whimpering and the feel of her body underneath my trembling.

"Sugar mommy, sweet as fuck." I give her one last peck then get off of her. Going back to her bathroom to put on my clothes, I headed back into her room to find her passed-out snoring. I didn't know what all she had needed but I found a big duffle bag that looked like it belonged to her bitch ass baby daddy. I packed her underclothes and a couple of shirts and pants. I'd buy her toiletries and whatever else she needed for her daughter.

I would have carried her out to my car but didn't want to make her more uncomfortable. I woke her up, helped her get dressed and told her to grab her purse. The whole ride to my extra place that I had tucked away she drifted off and was sleeping soundly.

* * *

I FINALLY MADE it to my house and didn't want to even go in. I had already seen multiple cars parked right in front of my driveway and knew it was my family. Thinking that I had been pulling a quick one over my dad, he was much wiser. I should have known that he wasn't going to go to my other place.

Hopping out of my car, I hit the locks and made it up to my porch. Before I could use my key, Lakendra was already opening the door smiling wide as hell, like she was excited and happy to see me. Lakendra was bad as fuck; she could've been a model with the way her body was set up.

She was at least five foot eight, long, slender legs. High cheek bones with slanted tight eyes. She had the nose that people in Hollywood paid to have. She kept her hair in nice small braids and was slim-thick with most of her weight hitting her thighs and ass with a flat stomach. I remember when I was so in love with her, now when I eyed her all I saw was pity.

"Hey Bo." She pulled me into a tight needy hug. I didn't want to hurt her feelings, so I placed my arms around her and pulled her in. Releasing her, I pushed past the foyer. I missed my house, it was massive in size, my front room was all white with gold pieces here and there.

Stepping out of my shoes, I made my way to my man cave, which was the family room that I turned into my own kick it spot.

Entering my man cave, I leaned against the door frame and just chuckled lowly. My father always violated when it came to respecting his kids' privacy. I couldn't even be mad because I was the one out of all his kids that pushed his patience to the limit. Second to me came my big sister Mattea.

I could only get away with so much, ignoring my family for over a month hadn't been on my agenda. Before I knew it time started to pass me by. My hands were constantly in a lot of shit. Ream and Solo had me running things so they could focus and tend to their families, on top of running illegal shit, I had legal things with my money tied into that I had to give lots of attention to.

I'd be so busy, and sleep deprived that I didn't have enough time for the people that loved and cared deeply about me.

"My wife, my beautiful fucking wife, has bags under her muthafuckin' eyes. Stressing and worrying about what her oldest son is doing. Worrying about your mental and a list of other things when it comes to you." My father's voice was too calm, that meant he was raging on the inside. Looking at him was like looking at myself in the mirror, my father didn't have dreads like me, but we looked like twins except my father was built bulkier.

"You sure you're not worried?" I smirked and stepped all the way into the room. My eyes landed on Mattea, she gave me a smug smile and gave me her middle finger on the sly.

"Is a pigs pussy beef?" My father tapped his left foot hard on my tiled floor. I had to stop fucking with his nerves or he would snap, my mother wasn't here to save me, and Mattea was the wrong person to take her place because she would egg my old man on. See my mother had this calm nurturing effect on my father. She could calm him by simply looking at him or touching his shoulder.

"I'm in here, Michael." He touched his forehead for emphasis. "Don't shit concerning my grown ass kids get past me. Just like I know how you have taken a liking to another mental patient like yourself." Fire ignited in my chest, I swallowed down my spit and clutched my fist then unclutched them immediately not wanting to send an unclear message to my father. Any indication of me wanting to get buck he'd push at it until he jumped right into action.

"You out here playing captain save a hoe. How the fuck can two people that don't have it all in their heads collide and become something."

"That's my business! I thought I told you not to fucking spy on me." I felt myself snapping as my father tauntingly tilted his head to the side.

"I start spying when you start ducking and dodging me. Do you know who the fuck I am lil nigga!" He stood up and Mattea's eyes got big. I looked into my father's wild eyes and didn't blink.

"You use the same muthafuckas that I use to use to dig for

information. Anytime you pay them they inform me!" He slammed his hands on his chest.

"You not gone play with me like I'm not that nigga that'll slap fire from yo raggedy ass."

"And you won't stand where I piss, shit, and fuck at talking to me like I'm still getting an allowance from you Beast." Mattea stood up and by now it felt like it was two against one. *Fuck them, take them the fuck out!*

"I can't! He's my fucking father and that's my sister!" I roared then ran towards the nearest wall and kicked it in. My foot got stuck in I fell in the middle of my rage. I scrambled to my feet and started punching the wall wishing it was somebody's face that I was smashing in.

"Still answering to that voice, you need help Michael. What is telling you to kill me and your sister?" My father's voice softened but I was too blinded by being pissed with this fuckin' voice in my head asking me to do bullshit. Why couldn't it leave me the fuck alone. I hated being portrayed as fucking nutty. I didn't want to hear voices; I didn't want to feel abnormal either.

"Let us help you, Michael." The smug look my sister had when I came in was now a sad look. I turned away and hit the wall once more. Feeling out of breath and defeated I leaned my forehead against the wall and allowed my tears to fall. My head was pounding, fist throbbing in pain.

My father walked up and touched my shoulder, and my body went stiff as that voice roared in my head. Ignoring it enough to listen to my father's words.

"I don't want help, I want y'all to let me live my fucking life. I ain't taking no crazy pills. My conscious get the best of me and I fuck up from time to time. I'm not a fucking kid, I don't need y'all baby-sitting me." I gritted.

"Michael, you don't have a choice baby." I turned

towards the door and looked into my mother's eyes. "You run from us because you know we know what you battle heavy with. I don't agree with how your father goes about trying to get through to you. Invading your privacy is disrespectful and next time he won't do it again." My father grunted and walked away from me; he plopped down on the couch as my mother approached me smelling like lavender.

"You don't want a repeat of what you did to Lakendra do you? Your father says you met a girl and she suffer from bipolar disorder." She looked over at my dad and gave him and hard stare. My mom didn't like when me and my father looked into people's backgrounds without their consent.

"You keep Lakendra around and leave her room to think she has some form of hope with you. Even after what you did and what she did to you. You two should be history. She shouldn't be here, or you shouldn't be here. How can you move on to something else when you have Lakendra here waiting for you. You've apologized time and time again to her, you're never here at home and I know that cause when you don't answer my phone, I call her, and she sadly says you never come home anymore. Honey, that girl is still hopeful and still in love. I want you to make it clear to her. First you need to get the proper help, your father knows all about hearing voices and listening to them when he shouldn't. You have to separate that voice and understand that it's a sickness that you don't have to listen to." She cupped my face in her soft hands and stroked my cheeks with her thumbs.

"Unless you want to make it work with Lakendra."

"I don't love her anymore." I never said that out loud. Lakendra was my first love, the first woman to break my heart although I was the one to break hers first. The saying that men couldn't take the same medicine was true. I couldn't take the fact that although I cheated, Lakendra got even but took it far by fucking one of my enemies while she was pregnant with my first born.

I lost control that night and did some shit I still regret to this day. All I know is that day I wasn't myself, something had taken over me.

"Mattea already talked to Ream and Solo." I could see the disdain in my mother's voice. She didn't like the illegal shit that I was out here doing but she accepted the fact that she couldn't change it. "You can take time off, so that we can help you get right. You have to visit Ms. Scott so she can diagnose you properly again then get you on the proper medication." I noticed my mom on her tippy toes struggling to hold onto my face, so I bowed in front of her to help her out.

I didn't want her hurting herself, she had metal in her hip and already walked with a slight limp.

"I can't momma, I don't want to be off pills." I looked away then back at her hating to tell her no.

"You ain't got a fucking choice! Don't tell my wife no-"

"Beast please!!!! Shut it up!" My mom let my face go and clapped her hands.

"Ma, that's not fair! Daddy locked me in a room and made me get help! So, Michael doesn't get to decide!" Mattea interjected as my mom offered my sister an icy look making her shut her mouth.

"Michael, come home just for a couple of days so we can get you help. Please baby." I sighed hard and slowly nodded my head. I was only going because I truly couldn't defy my mother to her face. To get them all off my back, I turned to walk out my man cave agreeing to go.

SOULFUL HURTZ

Lately, I had been feeling like I'm not meant for love. I didn't want it to define my path because I was doing well and thriving in my life hard. Looking over at my wife, that yearning disappeared. I used to yearn for her all the time, I wanted to make her happy because in my eyes she was the most beautiful woman walking besides my sisters.

I regretted walking down the aisle with her, making her my top priority. I wanted to communicate and get us back right, but every time I looked in Jocelyn's eyes, I could tell her attention and wants were on something other than me. Shit just felt forced, either I was lacking something, or she just wasn't feeling a nigga no more.

"What's wrong Hurtz?" Her pretty voice had me looking over at her in despair. I never wanted to be the nagging ass nigga that complained all the time. I tried my best to go with the flow.

"Got a lot going on today. Coach worked us like crazy in practice, I don't even feel up to having this party today either." That was the truth, my muscles hurt like shit and my mind wasn't on celebrating a birthday.

"Don't go then, I'm pretty sure they won't mind just coming to you." Jocelyn slid out of bed. I wondered if she even remembered that today was my fucking birthday.

"Convenient as fuck for you," I mumbled loud enough for her to hear me. Taking her slender frame in, I frowned. Jocelyn used to have a little thickness to her now she looked like she was nothing but skin in bones. Despite her looking skinny as hell, she still held her youthfulness beauty to her.

"Always sounding like your last name." She mumbled back over her shoulder. I ignored that jab, I wasn't hurting like I used to, I was just tired of her bullshit. Not wanting to back down like a buster ass nigga I said some shit that had her stopping in her tracks.

"It's always another someone that's willing to do what your mate can't seem to grasp."

"What the fuck is that supposed to mean." She put her hand on her peanut butter waist and gave me a daring look.

"It means you slacking bad as fuck Jah, you act like you got a list of things to do around here as my wife. I bet you ain't even planning on being there today for my dinner party." I threw the covers off and sat at the edge of the bed.

"My best friend is having a party today; you knew about this already. I've been talking about it for weeks now." She sighed hard and it was like I was getting a way better view of the real Jocelyn. It was a hard blow to the gut too. It was evident as fuck that Jocelyn didn't give a damn. All these years that we have been together, I constantly tried to make things easy for her.

I never wanted her to feel overwhelmed with Luv or Passion, so she never did a thing when it was regarding my sisters. I didn't fault her for that shit because in my mind it wasn't her responsibility. Today was my birthday though, and even though I wasn't that thrilled about it. It bothered me that she still hadn't even offered up a happy birthday or some form of acknowledgment. I knew about her best friend, Jessica's party, but I thought she would pick me over her friend since I was her husband that gave her any and everything she wanted.

"Yup." I stood up and started gathering my shit to go into the guest bathroom. I wanted to see what my sisters were up to and also see if they needed extra spending money to get themselves something nice to wear for my dinner party.

"Are you thinking about cheating on me, Soulful." I turned with my clothes in my hands and looked deep into her eyes.

"I wouldn't cheat on you Jah. I love you too much to do you foul like that." I could see the relief washing over her entire pretty face.

"What I would do, if I ever thought about cheating or knew I was close to cheating… I'd divorce you and make sure that you were straight even without me. I don't know what's up with you Jah, I haven't been able to get close to your heart ever since your brother got killed. That shit changed who you were. I never let my personal and hurtful problems get in the way of how I treat you, especially since you're my wife." I left out of the room and left her alone with her thoughts.

I didn't have it in me to argue or go back and forth with her today, because that shit drained me and made me feel like throwing the towel in. Back in the day, nobody could tell me that Jocelyn wasn't my dream girl. I crushed on her hard as fuck and was deeply in love with her. I'm the nigga that took her virginity and taught her everything that she knew.

I feel like the money changed who she was, she had the

money thanks to me and was free to do whatever with that money to make her happy. It was like she didn't look to me for happiness, her happiness was me giving her that almighty dollar to do as she pleased. I was the type of nigga that let a person do what they'd rather do. I didn't like asking a person for shit not even a helping hand.

After taking a much-needed shower, I threw on some basketball shorts and a white beater and walked into the kitchen since the smell coming from that area had my stomach growling. Luv was standing there stirring the pot while Passion sat bobbing her head listening to music through her air pods. When they noticed me walking in the kitchen, they both got super dramatic.

"Happy birthday Teddy!" Passion and Luv yelled out and rushed me. I can't even lie that shit made me feel so good that I was getting ready to shed a tear. My sisters were like my kids, I'd been taking care of them their whole lives. The task wasn't an easy one, but I got that shit done and was still doing the best I could to be their provider.

"Thank you, babies." I cleared my throat and took a seat at the kitchen table.

"Teddy, I got some fly shit for tonight!" Luv was the first to talk, I usually got on her about her language, but the girl had been cursing since she learned how to walk.

"You don't got to get extra'd out Luv, it's just a dinner party." I reminded her, Luv was eighteen, but she was going to have me growing gray hairs soon. I just turned twenty-six, but Luv had me feeling like I was way older than that with the way she constantly stressed me. Luv was really the loud and wild sister. Passion was fifteen and very quiet and sneaky.

Luv was outspoken and hardheaded, she loved to challenge me the most. Passion would listen and keep quiet and if she disobeyed me, she went about the shit in a sneaky way.

"Uncle Berto said, he going all out for you tonight! He said he wasn't gone let you spend this birthday acting like an old man. I just know he rented out some real player shit for you so trust and believe we getting lit tonight." I almost spit my orange juice out. Clearing my throat, I shook my head at Luv as she walked around the island and brought me my plate of food.

Luv did most of the cooking and I appreciated that. She learned how to cook from Sovereign. She started cooking little shit at fourteen and now she was a mini five-star chef. I looked at my plate and dug right in. She made buttermilk waffles with eggs, sausage, and bacon. Even though it was just an average breakfast the display of it had me feeling like I was in an expensive restaurant.

"Luv, I don't think I'm going out tonight. Just the dinner baby girl," I reassured her. To my understanding, Roberto's crazy ass wasn't even out here. He was supposed to be back in Mexico taking care of his cartel. He told me he had encountered a couple of problems back home that needed his attention.

Luv and Passion thought I missed the sly look that they gave each other.

"What's up with y'all?" I eyed them suspiciously. Love was getting ready to answer me until her phone started ringing. That was Passion's cue to give her focus back to her phone.

"Teddy, Uncle Berto wants to know if your wife wished you a sweet happy birthday." I felt my stomach turning. Roberto was probably about to do some wild ass shit. I wanted to lie in front of the girls and tell him she did. I didn't like lying though, that shit didn't settle good in my spirit.

"It's only nearing nine thirty. You know it takes time for her to warm up in the morning." Luv placed him on speaker.

"Well, happy birthday brotherrrrr! Tonight, we getting ratchet for thattttttt!" he clicked his teeth and chuckled into the phone.

"Ju first gift is outside right about now, go see and Luv record him for me please so I can have a good laugh." I could hear the stress in his voice. Whenever the cartel seemed to be stressing Roberto, he'd let it be known or his distance would let us all know that shit was rough back in Mexico.

I took the phone from Luv and took it off speaker. Walking out the kitchen and into my den, I told Roberto that I was now alone and asked him if he was straight.

"Of course, I'm okay. It's nothing major that my all-pink Ak-forty-seven can't fix chile. Now stop worrying about me and go give Luv the phone so she can record you." Letting it go and not pressing him for information, I walked back into the kitchen shaking my head at Roberto. I was kind of scared to see what he got for me this year.

The nigga had more money than me, so he never came up short when it came to him gifting me with things I didn't really need.

I took another bite of my food and walked towards the front of my house. Opening the door, I smiled big at the all-green Lamborghini parked right in front. A couple of seconds later a Lincoln Limousine pulled up, the driver stepped out first and opened the back door. Two blindfolded big booty strippers stood next to each other holding up signs that said, "What one wife won't do, a million side chicks would love to do." I looked around hoping Jocelyn was still getting dressed for the day so she couldn't see what was taking place.

About five other big booty strippers got out the car, two were topless and the others had thongs with pink stickers barely covering their nipples. I couldn't help but chuckle and smile big because Roberto was sick as fuck with it. The music played and I couldn't even believe the lyrics.

"I'm out of town, thuggin' with my rounds! My coochie pink, my booty hole brown! Where the niggas? Come looking for the hoes! Quit playing nigga, come suck a bitch toe!"

The strippers' asses were popping effortlessly with their hands on their knees as Luv start jumping and dancing singing the raunchy lyrics to "Pound town" By Sexy Red. The stripper who I assumed as the leader did the splits, making her booty jump to the beat had me in a trance. These females were cornfed and it amazed me how they were even able to do all of this with blindfolds on.

The blindfold idea had to come from Roberto, so they wouldn't know the location of my home. I took my attention off the strippers and could see three big body Benzes coming up the driveway. The first person to jump out was Roberto and I dropped my head at what this nigga had on. His wild hair wasn't in a ponytail today the shit was out blowing in the wind like crazy. This nigga had on an all-pink short set tuxedo; the shorts stopped above his knees with a light pink vest that looked too tight.

He had on all-pink Gucci socks that stopped below his knee, and to top his outfit off, he rocked a long mink pink coat that swept the dirty ground. His neck, ears and wrist were shining. That silly smirk on his face looked pleased to see the strippers getting ratchet for me. Sovereign hopped out the second Benz with balloons as one of her guards popped the trunk pulling out lots of designer bags.

I couldn't even deny how good they made me feel, to see my family turn up and happy to celebrate a special day had me feeling high and I hadn't even smoked any weed.

"Pound town! Just left pound town! With my nigga, he

just took a bitch down! Yeah, that nigga dick a bitch down! Yeah, that nigga eat me out!" Roberto started dancing with the strippers, popping the rubber bands to his bankroll of money. Throwing it up in the air, letting the money rain all over them.

I couldn't move from my spot on the porch because by now I'm sure Jocelyn was somewhere watching, and I didn't want to disrespect her. I appreciated the fuck out of the strippers and the way their asses were moving. Sovereign made her way to my steps with her security right behind her. She pointed towards my open door, and they walked past us, to put all my gifts inside the house.

"Happy birthday, Teddy. Roberto beat me with the gifts this year but we celebrating all day." She grabbed me for an embrace, and I hugged her tight, happy that she always came through for me no matter what.

"Good looking sis, you know I appreciate everything y'all do for me even though I feel like it's too much man." That was the truth, real fucking family of mine. Sovereign and Roberto always went the extra mile for me. I appreciated them so much, no questions asked, I lay my life down for them. We watch Roberto who now had his hands on his hips as a stripper clapped her ass on him.

"That's right Uncle Berto! Get that shit for thatttttt!!!!" Luv was too pumped up, more excited than me. The funny part about it was Roberto couldn't dance to save his life. He loved dancing but was always offbeat.

The horrible song finally went off and the strippers retreated back inside of the limousine with the help of Roberto and the driver.

"Luv, come help pick up all this money for the girls." Roberto was out of breath fanning himself.

"Wheeewww, I need a drank!" He slapped my shoulder and told me happy birthday. I took a long look at the new whip he bought and nodded my head. It was on my list of things to get after I won the Superbowl, I should've known once I mentioned it, Roberto was going to buy it.

We all went back inside the house and sat in the living room, reflecting and laughing at Roberto.

"Di one stripper with cellulite all over her booty, had me in love! I mean that's all real ass. I need to get her information and make her a wife for that!" He was serious, but it made me laugh because Roberto love dsaying, "For that" To make his point clear. He said the shit so much he had my sisters and Sovereign saying it.

"See this Chica ain't hitting on shit with those cheap name brand clothes and shoes she got ju. I got ju a Lamborghini truck, dropped two hundred thousand. I wipe my ass with that, for that!" He snapped his fingers as Sovereign pulled out her iPad out of her purse with a sneaky look. These two loved outdoing each other in everything, especially when it came to gifts. Most of the time it was too overwhelming, I felt like the little brother stuck inside of the big siblings' competitions.

"Teddy, I did out do this ass clapping bitch." Roberto fake grabbed at his neck and gasped hard like he was offended. Fanning himself dramatically with his long French tip nails, he flicked her off then rolled his eyes. Sovereign asked for the remote to my TV then tapped at her iPad until it was mirroring my TV.

The first picture that popped up had my mouth drying up, as she jumped up and danced a little with a big grin on her face. I was lost for words as she spoke.

"Me and hubby dropped big, big M's for thatttttt!!!" She

looked over at Roberto as he gagged, and looked on with a big smile.

"French style Chateau mansion baby with a big ass pool in the front and in the mutha fuckin back. We had to upgrade you!"

"Queen, you know I can't take this." She smacked her lips as I shook my head no.

"You can use this for you, Inferno and the kids." I stated seriously.

"Don't disrespect me! Inferno and I just had a new mansion built. You know my baby likes burning shit, so our shit is set up perfectly for him. What you don't like it?" She frowned and I quickly stood to my feet and hugged her to show my appreciation.

"Awww! I'm still mad for that but I love y'all let me get in on the love." Roberto put his arms around both of us. Breaking apart, I wiped at my tears.

"Damn, ju cry more than me." Roberto laughed but I didn't find shit funny.

"Y'all always tryna hoe me up, making me all emotional." I sat down just as Jocelyn was walking down the steps. Her brown skin glowed, instead of wearing her eyeglasses, she had on contacts.

I could never get over how beautiful Jah was, it looked like she was going to the gym. She had a Nike sports bra and short spandex on.

"Hey sis-in-law!" Roberto smirked, tossing his hair behind his shoulders and shimming. This nigga was sometimes over the top animated, but he got really dramatic when he knew somebody didn't like him. Sovereign remained silent, she was always quiet when she didn't care for a person and knew she couldn't kill them. That's the thing Jocelyn didn't understand, she talked slick all the time to people that appeared nice and chill. What she didn't know is that these same people killed muthafuckas for small things and went on and life like it was nothing. They only dealt with and respected her because of me.

The tension was super thick it would take a saw to cut through it. Jocelyn didn't respond so Roberto kept at it, he wasn't going to accept her blatant disrespect.

"What's the tea sis?" Roberto sat up a little and I gave him a warning look to let her be. When Jocelyn made it to the door, she turned to face all of us with a disgusted look on her face.

"I'm no sister-in-law of yours, a real brother-in-law wouldn't bring hoe ass stripping bitches in front of my house for my husband!" She stepped away from the door just as I rubbed my hands down my head, getting ready to deal with Jocelyn feeling slighted.

"How would you feel if one of my friends brought a bunch of big dick niggas in front of our home, Soulful." She whined. "This why I don't like your little fake ass family." Sovereign clicked her teeth and sat up in the lazy boy chair she was occupying.

"Jocelyn, watch yourself. I wouldn't want you to get hurt. You understand right?" Sovereign voice had an icy chill to it. Nothing in her eyes was welcoming.

"Ain't nothing fake about us, you know that. Don't be a fool baby girl." Sovereign reached back into her Chanel bag and pulled out a cigar. She was beginning to act just like her husband Inferno.

"Instead of running off at the mouth and out of the house, why don't you go make your husband a drink and bring me one while you're at it. I let you be around me because I love Teddy. I'm sure you know that I will kill, whoop a bitch and do a lot of other things for him. You know?" Once her cigar was lit, she crossed her legs.

"Have you told your husband happy birthday? What have you done Jocelyn? Maybe if you did more, then... Roberto here wouldn't have to get big booty, blindfolded strippers to do your job." Sovereign chuckled hard and Jocelyn gave me a hurt look then stormed out, making sure to slam the door on her way out. She wanted to be seen, our cars weren't even parked out front. We kept them in the garage. She would be making a bigger fool out of herself walking around our massive home just to get to the back to let her car out.

I looked over at Sovereign and she shrugged and crossed her legs.

"I guess she's not going to get me that drink. Damn, Teddy you need a Butler. You too rich to be acting like you still in the hood. Roberto, go get me a damn drink. You know if it was Teddy's wife, I'd slap the fucking fire out of her disrespectful mouth." Sovereign gritted and mumbled other things underneath her breath.

"I guess I'll get a drink, but I'm not a butler for that! I'm just going because I need one too. That wife of yours… Ju need to fuck her and fuck her well. She acts like she needs dick in her life." Roberto walked out making sure to let his pink mink coat drag behind him.

I put my face in my hands because Jocelyn picked today out of all days to act like a bitch. She would be getting dick, if she stayed her ass at home for once. Always wanting to be seen popping out and partying. My wife brought more attention to the blogs than I did and that said a lot since I was the star of my team.

"Stop giving CPR to some shit that can't be revived. I'm not gon' tell you what you should do because you grown. However, time is really precious in this lifetime. We love who we love and that's real. Don't let your loyalty cause you to betray yourself. Now think hard on that." Sovereign remained quiet and so did I. I let her words marinate in my head, as each second passed by, the reality of her words became clearer.

ERA

I loved when we had a high roller coming through the restaurant. We shut down the entire place three hours before closing time since quarterback star Soul Hurtz and his family were coming through. I hand-picked my staff tonight, of course I let Praylah and my other close friend Ju'well stay along with a couple of other loyal employees that did their jobs with no complaints.

"When we done here, we need to go to the strip club!" Ju'well was super pretty, men tried their best to holler at her, but she was a hundred percent lesbian. Like me, she had got her heart broken only but once and decided that all men were the same. She has been gay for six years and loved her lifestyle. The funny part about it though was women were almost just as worse as men.

Ju'well stayed taking females bitches and didn't give a damn about it. She was a curvy plus size beauty with a shape a lot of us plus size women would die for. All of her weight went straight to her hips, ass, and breast. Her chinky eyes made her alluringly beautiful.

"You know I don't have anything to wear." I looked at my best friend and rolled my eyes. Praylah had pissed me off, I didn't know that Jarei was really that abusive the way that he was. While I was happy that Mr. Brownston took a liking to her and helped her out. I wanted to be there for her too. She could have stayed with me, her and my god daughter. I wanted to find Jarei and get him fucked up for dogging my best friend the way he had.

Praylah was one of those girls that deserved the entire universe and then more. She was always looking out and trying to help and understand people that didn't even deserve it. I didn't want Praylah getting out of a relationship then taking another man very serious so soon. She wore her heart on her sleeve and gave everyone the benefit before seeing the reasons for doubt.

Mr. Brownston seemed cool, but he was abnormally weird to me. Very handsome but sometimes when I looked into his eyes it was like I was staring into the eyes of a demon. I ignored the rumors about him really being crazy and murdering people.

At the end of the day, he was my boss and I made damn good money working for not just one but multiple franchises that he owned. I've been throwing my all into work because I knew my singing career was over now that me and Devin were done. Devin called every single day and left long voice mails. Some were him calling and begging while others were him calling me all kinds of fat bitches. I was close to changing my number like Praylah and moving forward.

I was grateful that Devin hadn't taken things a step further by popping up at my place.

"I'm pretty sure both of y'all got something to wear. Praylah don't even search that brain of yours for excuses because we both the same size. You can come to my house and try some stuff on." I was wishing Ju'well luck with getting Praylah to come out and have fun.

"Heaven supposed to be back with me tomorrow." I smacked my lips because Praylah parents loved having Heaven. Praylah normally would pick Heaven up late in the evening so she could join her parents for dinner.

"Excuse me ladies, sorry to intrude." I looked up and stared into the eyes of a very handsome Hispanic guy, he had his hair down looking like he had just wet it. The silk, pink Versace shirt was unbuttoned and opened showing his chest and abs. He was pretty as hell and he smelled expensive; I couldn't name the perfume he had on, but I made a mental note to ask him. I think we all were stunned by his appearance; I've seen a lot of gay men but this one standing before me was sexy as hell and without even saying much you could feel his powerful presence.

"I'm Roberto. My brother will be here in about fifteen minutes. After the food is served, I got him a special cake. I wanted to know if one of you chicas could sing. I'll pay you, to do that for my brother. His wife is such a bitch and I want to get his mind off her, he's gone through enough and deserves to smile." He dug into his light tan pants and pulled a knot of money out and held it out like he was presenting a prize to us.

"Era can sing!" Ju'well blurted out making me snap my eyes towards her.

"Era, sing for my Hermano? Si?" Roberto smiled and I couldn't see myself saying no to him or that knot full of money that sat perfectly in his hands.

"Your brother is Soulful Hurtz right?" At the mention of his name, Roberto eyes smiled confirming just that. I've seen lots of speculation in the blogs. First, they accused Roberto as being Soulful's secret boyfriend then they start saying how Soulful had ties with the cartel because of Roberto.

"Si, that's my Hermano." He stood well poised as if he was unbothered by being connected to one of the best quarterbacks in the NFL.

"Okay, I'll do it." Roberto surprised me by walking right up to me and hugging me tight. His skin was so soft, and he smelled like an exotic flower.

"If I didn't have a wife and a husband, I'd take you back to Mexico and marry ju. Your skin is so hermosa and ju have a top shelf stacked booty." I giggled still enjoying his smell. He tapped the top of my ass boldly and walked out. Me and my girls just looked at each other and fell out laughing.

"I'd fuck him." Ju'well shrugged. "Nah, I'd probably let him eat me though!" We laughed as Ju'well said she was just kidding but behind that, I saw the seriousness in her eyes. Roberto was fine, I just wasn't interested in a bisexual man.

"Let's get to work, I can already hear guest inside. The chefs should be almost done preparing the food and-" I looked at Praylah who had a distant look on her face. "What's wrong Praylah?"

"Nothing, still adjusting to the new two front teeth in my mouth. Then for some reason, Michael hasn't shown up. I mean, I understand he told me that he didn't want anything from me and that I could pay him rent. He hasn't even collected that from me. I have a car and that came from him along with the pink slip, he had someone drop it off at the place me and Heaven been staying at. Still no call or anything from him. It feels weird." I hated to see that cloudy look in my best friend's eyes.

"Come on, let's go to my office. The servers can handle

the first half." We left out of the kitchen area and headed towards my office space that was actually plush and very comfortable. My office space made me feel like a CEO, I really appreciated being able to relax and being comfortable at work. This restaurant could sometimes get busy and whenever I needed to clear my mind, my office space was my sanctuary to do so.

I had a big desk and a long and wide sectional couch. Mr. Brownston didn't spare any expenses when it came to the high-end furniture and design of the place. I took a seat behind my desk while Praylah and Ju'well sat on the couch. I eyed Praylah for a while as she messed around with her fingers. Cringing at the fact that she had started back biting her nails, I cleared my throat to get her attention.

"Praylah?"

"Hmm?" She gave me those big innocent eyes.

"Did you fuck Mr. Brownston?" I got straight to the point with a small smirk on my face. Her cheeks turned red as she blushed and nibbled on her bottom lip.

Slapping my hands against the table, my mouth fell open.

"Oh my goodness! Pray!" I whined out as Ju'well started laughing.

"I mean, come on friend! The nigga is scary looking but fine as hell. So, what if she did!" I eyed Ju'well crazy ass and gave Praylah my attention. Praylah couldn't even fix her face to save her life. She looked like she had been caught doing some shit she shouldn't have been doing. Mr. Brownston crazy ass was one of those things she needed to stay the hell away from. I was kind of scared for her, the stories I heard from Devin and other people made me never want to cross or do anything wrong while running his restaurant.

"Umm, I didn't fuck him but, I uhhh… got my pussy ate

for the first time and it was the best feeling in my life. We kind of talked to each other about our personal problems and I felt like we connected on a deep level. He even said he wanted me but would wait until I fell out of love with Jarei. He's not pushing himself on me and I like that, but I do want to see and talk to him. He makes me feel safe and I fear that Jarei is going to pop up and find me and it's going to be bad like this last time." Her words trailed off; I got angry watching her be visibly shaken the fuck up.

I mean Praylah was literally trembling like she really feared this man. It made me emotional thinking about the years of abuse she endured and her suffering in total silence without getting me to help her. It also made me feel a way, like did she trust me? I told her all of my problems and she had always been there for me.

"Praylah, I don't want to sound selfish, but we supposed to be best friends. Why didn't you tell me? Why not go to the police or something, even your parents?" I searched her eyes swallowing down the small lump forming in my throat. I went along with the flow of things these past couple of weeks. I didn't want to make her relive anything or get depressed by me asking her so many questions. So much has happened that I just wanted to be there for her now.

I just had to have some answers now, even though it really wasn't the right time to know like that because we were at work.

"I liked it at one point, and actually believed half of the things he put into my head. You know, the bipolar shit that I go through, but you don't know the deep depression and me feeling worthless. So worthless and lazy that sometimes I don't even want to take care of myself. Shower or do the things that I'm supposed to do as a woman. I was embarrassed and I felt bad for Jarei because he ended up with a useless woman like me. Him hitting on me and talking to me like how he did sometimes make me feel alive when I would go in those dark places inside of my mind." She backhanded her tears as Ju'well draped her arm around her and pulled her close.

"I start taking medication and it made me better. If Jarei wasn't abusing me then I would be abusing myself. My mind, I don't know my mind felt weird and stuck on thinking that it was the proper way to live. You know? I get to feeling down and out and get fearful of going too far and not being a good mother to Heaven. I'd force myself to take medicine and then my mood will be good for work and parenting. Then I would keep that on repeat. You guys are like my family. I didn't want to put my craziness off on y'all then you both would start viewing me differently." She sadly looked away. I stood and walked around my desk, I squatted right in front of her and grabbed her hands.

"Praylah, I swear you my sister baby. I love you; we love you. That's what we here for, none of us about to sit up and judge you. Don't keep shit like that away from us, please." Although we both met Ju'well through working here we didn't view her any less. We had a strong bond, a sisterhood that kept us all a float.

"I love you guys too." Without having to say it we immediately embraced each other.

"I swear y'all always have me on some emotional shit." Ju'well wiped her eyes as we broke apart. "So, he at that poonannniiiii." She sang as Praylah blushed hard.

"Yes, and he ate it good. He kissed all on my belly and girl he washed between my funky ass cheeks." We all fell out laughing.

"Wait, he split those hefty cheeks of yours and like really

scrubbed that muthafucka?" Ju'well asked as I got up with a struggle for squatting down low for so long. I did not have Megan knees, so I felt the strain of sitting up. Plopping down on the sectional next to Praylah, I rubbed my knees.

"Yes, he soaped that towel up and really got between my filthy ass cheeks." Praylah's entire face was red now and she couldn't stop blushing.

"I'll sayyyyy, it's giving, he loves your filthy fuckin panties baby. Did he smell the towel when he was done?" I frowned my face up at Ju'well, she always took it too far.

"See bitch, you going to hell." I bust out laughing because the look on Ju'well face told me that her crazy ass was seriously asking and waiting for her question to be answered.

"I'm already going to hell but it's worth it chile. I love bumping coochies too much to stop. Now answer me, Praylah!" We couldn't stop laughing to save our lives, this is what I loved about us. We could be having a heart to heart then be laughing the next couple of seconds.

"I don't think he smelled the towel. My goodness, I hope he didn't smell the towel. I mean he was really deep in my booty scrubbing." She shivered like she had the chills. "The way he looks at me and how he talks to me, makes me feel a way y'all. I know I don't need a relationship anytime soon, but I just feel like he's something special." Her face got back serious.

"I hope I am something special." All of our eyes snapped in the direction of Mr. Brownston, like fire being attached to my ass, I hopped up and greeted him like a solider does its captain.

"Mr. Brownston, we came back here to uhh, go over some things for tonight's guest." He gave me a blank uncomfortable look then focused his gaze on Praylah. It was very weird because we all remained silent watching their stare off.

Without being told, Praylah stood and walked up to him. He placed his hand at the small of her back and kissed her temple, she laid her head on his chest like he was her savior.

"I'm here tonight, celebrating with my boy Soulful. I want you to come out with me tonight, you can bring your friends. I just want to chill with you, I missed you sugar mommy." Me and Ju'well looked at each other and smiled, I really wanted to laugh because why the fuck was he calling my best friend sugar mommy. All these years that I worked for him I never saw him so gentle with anyone.

"Okay and umm, I missed you too Michael." She placed her small hand on his chest, and I could see him inhale then exhale hard like her touch did something to him. Wait… did she just give us a hard time going out but now she was all game since he walked in? Did she just call Mr. Brownston aka Debo by his government. I was really standing her throwed the fuck off, but I loved this for her. I know I said they were moving too fast but shit if y'all could see the way my best friend and boss was looking right now, y'all would call it love at first sight.

"Era, it's time to sing happy birthday now." My stomach tightened as my mouth went dry. I wanted to be a celebrity and sing for millions of people. I didn't understand why now at this very moment, I felt myself freezing up and not really wanting to sing for Soulful. Each step that I took towards the door made me feel queasy. I made my way to the front of the restaurant clearing my throat, hitting high and low notes preparing myself to sing. My eyes landed on Soulful and in person, photos from social media did this man no justice.

Handsome was an understatement. Sitting in his chair looking nonchalant like he didn't too much care for all the attention to be on him. His butterscotch skin glowed under the lights, everything on him seemed perfect down to the crispy line up and waves covering his head. His massive hand closed around the entire glass cup as he knocked down whatever dark liquid that was inside of his cup. His eyes landed on me and stayed on me, my heart sped up and I couldn't believe that Soulful Hurtz had stolen my breath from a great distance.

SOULFUL HURTZ

My eyes feel heavy, it's starting to feel like it's a major struggle to keep them open. A couple of my teammates and friends sit around the table toasting and celebrating my birthday. Each time I look up at Sovereign or Roberto, I feel conflicted. A strong confliction regarding Jocelyn, she proved them right each time and also, she proved my assumptions right as well. This whole marriage has been a one-way street.

Truth was I always felt like I liked and then loved her way more than she did me. My mind wondered so much about Jocelyn that I struggled sitting at my own birthday dinner party; I was tired mentally and physically. I just wanted my wife here with me, I wanted her to show me that she gave a fuck. Looking at the time, it read seven, fifty-five. Even though she was upset with how the way things went down today. She still didn't offer me two words, happy birthday. Why the fuck was that shit so hard for her.

Did she loathe being with me? Was it the money that kept her posted up, sometimes acting like she was happy? Was she just too comfortable? I tried all type of shit that a nigga like me would never try to make it work. Dates, romantic dinners, my last resort that I tried months ago was marriage counseling. None of that shit worked. I loved Jocelyn too much to just kick her to the curb with nothing. Nothing was working, I didn't feel the spark the romance or nothing with her anymore.

This shit had me feeling drained and tired as fuck. I was ready to push on and move the fuck around. I didn't like this feeling like I was forcing some shit that didn't even have to be in the first damn place. She got jealous at the mention of me moving on but never did anything to try to make me feel like I should stay in this marriage. The way I saw it, we were both still young, not even in our thirties yet.

I didn't want a failed marriage under my belt, but it was looking like we both needed something different. Scanning the restaurant, I tuned out all the side conversations that was happening at the table and picked up my cognac and knocked it back. Tired of thinking about Jocelyn, I needed the perfect distraction.

As if God had answered my prayers, my eyes landed on a chocolate beauty that had a magnetic sensation traveling through me at a persistent pace. *Sexy as fuck!* I thought as my eyes fell to her wide hips, feeling like that was disrespectful, I gave her my eyes. Our gazes never wavered, I never blinked, and I don't think she did either.

"That's top shelf booty." I stopped looking at her and looked at Roberto, I don't know why I was feeling conflicted by his flirtatious remark towards the stranger female that was now getting closer to my table. I didn't like the fact that he was eyeing her the same way that I was a couple of seconds ago. I reminded myself that I was married and needed to let that shit go but then she started singing, sounding like

Jennifer Hudson. Her vocals were strong, and she held the fuck out of a note.

She demanded everyone with her voice to shut up and listen. All I knew right now was that nothing or no one seemed to matter at the moment but the sound of her voice. Her low soulful eyes fluttered and landed on me.

"Happy birthday, dear Soulful…Happy birthday to you!" She changed her voice and let it soar. Her smile shows in her eyes as she gives me those white perfectly aligned teeth. When her mouth turns upwards, I notice the small dimples in her chubby cheeks. The confidence in her posture as everyone claps and cheers as her posture remains upright. My eyes travel on their own and land on her perfect sized cantaloupe sized breast, mouthwatering, I can't stop eying her entire form that's now standing right before me.

That nervous girlie laugh shows that she was a little shy, but did she know the gift that she had. Why is she working at a restaurant when she should be on somebody's stage and making millions.

"The fuck wrong with you Soul?" My teammate snaps me out of my daze. I look at him with disgust only because I can see the white substance in his nose canal. I hated people that did hardcore drugs because it reminded me too much of my mother and how she selfishly didn't decide to get her shit together for me and my sisters. Drugs took her out of this world, so seeing anyone else ruining their selves had made me judgmental. Substance abuse was big in the NFL, coaches and team owners ignored that shit, as long as players did what they were supposed to do on the field.

Dion was cool when he wasn't on that shit, I invited my whole team and only a couple of them showed. Most niggas were just jealous and hated the fact that I was a star player. My name got a lot of buzz and because of that, niggas felt challenged like they were in some sort of competition. I let niggas beef with themselves, as long as they didn't push that shit my way disrespectfully. Dion and the niggas that came with him were cool to me, they never acted like they were jealous or like they had a problem. That was why they were here, the only thing I made clear was to never come around me high off a substance. I didn't rock with that shit at all.

"Go clean yo nose, my nigga. My sisters and family are here." He offered a remorseful look and stood to excuse himself. My eyes return to… "Era." I read her name tag allowed and everyone takes notice including her. Placing her eyes on me, I licked my lips and coolly complimented her but, on the inside, it felt like she had struck a match in the pit of my gut.

"Your voice is beautiful, so beautiful that I can't allow it to go to waste here at this restaurant. Not trying to offend you, Debo." I looked over at him and his eyes seemed to be somewhere else, he didn't even acknowledge what I said. It's like the nigga couldn't even here me, I followed where his eyes were, and they were focused on a light skin chick that looked to be the same height and size as Era.

Focusing back on her, she kept that beautiful smile on her face remaining professional and sexy as fuck. I wanted her to come closer so I could see what she smelled like. Fuck was wrong with me, deep down I knew I wouldn't disrespect my wife like that no matter how bad and far off we were. I just couldn't deny this magnetic organic pull that Era had on me.

"Shelby, she is a good friend of mine. She manages a few big artists in the industry. She used to be my publicist, until she gave all of her dedication to the industry and finding good talent. If you can give me your number, I can reach out to her and then shoot you a text with her information." I felt guilty as hell because I didn't know what other way to get her number. I didn't want this to be our last encounter for some reason. It felt like I needed to be connected to her in some type of way.

"Oh my gosh, that's so sweet of you." She neared me with a stunned expression. I lick my lips at her curvaceous silhouette approaching me. My dick reacts to the soft sweet scent her body reeks of. It was something about the confidence in her eyes as she pulled a pin from the pocket on her shirt. She cautiously reached for the napkin careful not to bump into me as she wrote her digits down on the napkin.

Her natural aura is intriguing, and it makes a nigga want to get to know her immediately. The uniform she is wearing ain't doing shit for her, it's like her curves are hard as hell not to notice. Her hips are wide as hell, and I love the way it's well portioned to her waist that dips in a little.

Her smell so fucking intoxicating and alluring that I smell it even though now she's across the room looking over the other employees as they bring smaller plates for the cake that another woman is now cutting into to prepare to serve. She flutters around the restaurant and my eyes gravitate to wherever she lands, hoping that she comes back over her and bless me with her presence again.

Feeling like I need to take the edge off, I knock back a shot then pick up my cold iced water to cool myself off and hopefully get my hard dick to go the fuck down.

"Shelby huh?" Sovereign got my attention; she gave me a pestering smile and shook her head. "Careful Teddy, us big girls are on a whole other level than what you seem to be used to. Once you go plus, going slim is slim to not happening again." She tilted her champagne flute back then pulled out one of her cigars as Inferno chuckled and lit it for her.

"Sovereign is right lil bro, you got the same look that I

had for Sove. Same look that I give a new fire that I ignite for the first time in my basement." He eyed the torch that he used to light Sovereign's cigar without looking up at me. I shook my head and smiled because I had been caught. Even my sisters were looking at me with heavy curiosity.

"I mean, do you really want to be the type that tells people that their wife can't cook a meal for them?" Roberto looked at Inferno and chuckled, picking up his champagne flute he took a sip then placed the glass back down.

"Shut the fuck up Berto." Inferno looked over at his brother as I looked on in confusion but then it hit me what Roberto was getting at. Inferno didn't allow Sovereign to cook for niggas at all. Whenever we came to their house, he had his chefs' cook instead of her. He let it be known that his wife could only cook meals for him. I remember him saying that another man tasting his wife cooking was like knowing and getting a good insight to how good her pussy was.

Sovereign food was only reserved for her and the kids with Inferno at the top of the list. We all fell out laughing as the waiter started placing slices of cakes in front of us.

"I'm going to get going Teddy." Luv stood up as I looked at her suspiciously.

"Take Passion with you, I'll be home late." I didn't want to go home no time soon; I didn't even want to see Jocelyn at all.

"Teddy, I was supposed to go meet with my friends." She pouted and I gave her a hard look.

"Like I said take Passion and drop her off at home and while you're there change your clothes. Don't make me come out looking for you Luv, be home at a decent time. I will be checking the cameras." She nodded her head and hugged Sovereign and Roberto then me, Passion did the same before they were headed out.

Happy that Luv didn't give me a hard time by trying to debate me in front of everyone, I scanned the restaurant and disappointment hit me when I couldn't locate Era.

"Her and my girl should be coming to the club with us tonight." Debo finally spoke up, never looking up from his phone. I guess his comment was directed towards me, he must've seen me looking thirsty searching the place high and low for Ms. Chocolate sensation. I wouldn't take anything to the level of disrespect, hopefully I wouldn't. I couldn't even remember the last time I even got some pussy from my busy ass wife.

* * *

THE CLUB WAS PACKED and no surprise, half of the people here already heard from the blogs that I would be out celebrating my birthday in Hollywood. I sat all the way in the cut, the lights were dim, and the music was so loud that I could feel that shit in my chest. I drank Dusse from the bottle and bobbed my head and chuckled every couple of seconds, Roberto was drunk and acting a fool with the strippers.

He was more prepared than all of us, he had two suitcases being guarded by his security. I believed the nigga when he said he had his accountant get him over a million dollars in ones for tonight. Our section's entire floor was full of money covering the seats and floor. Strippers of all nationalities kept coming in rotation to make their money. I had my own ones that I casually tossed in the air making it rain.

I felt the effects of the liquor and didn't really know what to do with myself. Sovereign had excused herself along with Inferno. Now it was just me, Roberto and Debo who didn't really seem like he was interested in the club scene. Debo had brought a stud chick that he introduced as Honor with him she was real cool and her and Roberto clicked immediately. Era and her friends were on the dance floor which was good for me. I already reasoned with myself that I needed to stay far away from her.

Era had put on some shit that had all these niggas in the club oogling the fuck out of her. Her curvaceous frame was insane, the way her short white dress kept riding up her thighs and cupping her ass each time she bent over and twerked.

"Yo Debo, who the chick with your girl?" I looked up as Honor picked up a napkin and wiped the sweat from her face. A stripper walked over to us and gave us her ass as she dropped it down low and twerked. I threw a stack of money in the air and watched it rain down all over her.

"Ju'well." Debo said as his eyes remained on the dance floor at the girl, I assumed he was into. He never stopped looking at her from the time we got in this bitch. It was like he was obsessed with watching her, I hoped that the niggas on the dance floor was smart enough to stay the fuck away from her. Debo name rang bells, he was well known and respected all across Los Angeles.

I also fucked with his street football team; Slaughter Gang gave back to the communities in need each summer. Debo was on some street legendary shit; he kept quiet most of the time, but he was a real ass nigga. That's all I liked to be surrounded by was real niggas. I remember when he approached me after one of my games years ago thanking me for winning him lots of money on a bet he placed on the Packers.

"Ju'well, I like that name, I think I'ma go get at her." Honor smiled; it still tripped me the fuck out how she looked just like a nigga with hella swag.

"Good, matter fact, tell all three of them to make their way over here." He smirked mischievously at me. "Ay, Era is a cool ass chick. They don't make females like her no more, she don't know it but I fuck with her heavy. Hard ass worker and she runs my franchise well. She a good look for you, my nigga. Just look into her so you can know the ins and out." He sat up and told the stripper something that I couldn't hear. She looked back sadly and fixed her G-string and walked away. I didn't plan on looking into Era because I didn't need to, I had a wife and wouldn't play Jocelyn like that even though she was treating a nigga like I wasn't shit.

Ten minutes passed by, and all three women were laughing and dancing in our section. They even had their own stacks of money and was slapping the strippers on the ass, having a good ass time. My eyes stayed on Era, the longer I watched her the harder my dick got. It was hard not to watch her; her skin was so fucking beautiful like God purposely covered her with dark chocolate to temp mankind into sinful thoughts of temptation.

Looking at the time, I noted that it was hitting on two in the morning. Roberto now had his shirt tied on top of his head sitting slumped with a bankroll still in his hand. A light skin stripper was licking all over his neck as he took a couple of sips from his Ace of Spades. Holding onto a handful of ass his eyes were low as fuck.

Debo was busy touching all over his girl and kissing her like they were in a high school make out session. I felt my own eyes getting lower as I leaned closer to Era. Feeling buzzed off the liquor and good I motioned for her to scoot closer to me. She smiled timidly as my eyes landed on her chocolate thighs. I don't know what was coming over me, but I whispered some corny shit in her ear. Her sexy voice sounded angelic, and it did something to my battered soul.

"Sing to me Era." I spoke clear right into her ear, placing my hand on her thick thigh, I felt her body get tense. Her skin felt like silk, and I couldn't help the motion of my hand rubbing in a circular motion against the smoothness of her skin. She sang happy birthday really low and soothingly in my ear and I no longer heard the loud club music playing. I no longer saw strippers and it didn't feel like I was surrounded by strangers in a packed club.

The more she sang in my ear the more intimate it was starting to feel. Her lips were so close that I could feel her breath tickling my skin. Turning my face slowly until my lips were connected with hers, I let my hands run up between her thick thighs and she opened them without any hesitation. My fingers moved her panties to the side, and I was greeted by her hot wet center. Thrusting her hips to position her clit right on the pad of my index finger, I stummed that muthafucka like it was a guitar and watched her eyes shut tight in ecstasy. Her sweet alcoholic tongue roamed my mouth, I grabbed a handful of ass and squeezed until she was gasping right in my mouth.

"You tryna get fucked Era?" All that loyalty shit went out the window, I was in a heap of heat. My dick was so damn hard that I couldn't concentrate on shit but the feeling of her contracting walls clenching down on my middle finger.

"Yesss Soulful." She whimpered and that was all the confirmation I needed. I stood up ignoring everything and everyone except for Era. I had to have her; I couldn't resist. The way that we connected with each other without knowing one another. I could blame it on my own intoxication or my wants overpowering my need to go the fuck home to my wife. Right now, all I could think about was the sweet taste of Era's pussy being right on my taste buds as I licked my fingers that was soaked with her essence.

I stood back and watched her talk with her friends and when she was done, I led her to the back of the club where my driver waited for me. I had a conscience, but I was overpowering it with justified thoughts. Jocelyn didn't tell me happy birthday, but Era sung that shit to me sweetly. Jocelyn wasn't at home because if she was there at three in the morning, she would have been calling me, finding it unusual for me not to be there.

I spent the entire ride to the hotel drinking and letting my hands roam Era. She felt so soft, her pussy so gushy and tempting, the way that she looked at me and moaned my name had my head feeling cloudy as fuck.

"I got to have you." I heard myself slurring. Yea, a nigga was tripping big time, I was in too deep to back out now.

SOULFUL HURTZ

I didn't need to be seen checking into a hotel in the middle of the night, so I gave my driver a stack of money and made him get the room for me. Once that was squared away, I had him drive me and Era around to the back as we walked in through the back and got right onto the elevator. We both remained quiet like we were lost in our own thoughts.

I didn't view her as a hoe even though she came with me to this room, and we didn't know much about each other. I got another vibe from her, and it was a wholesome one. Her eyes mirrored mine, the need that we had between each other was powerful and couldn't be denied even if we tried.

Taking my Versace shirt off first, I undid my jeans and just stared at her. It seemed like reality was starting to hit her when mine had left me since the moment we walked out of the club. Pulling my jeans off, my eyes never leave hers. Those beautiful deep set of brown eyes, she looked like a fucking special antique barbie doll, the kind that you would have to keep on a shelf. Too delicate to play around with because if you broke it, it couldn't be replaced.

Her expression as I remove my boxers makes me bite my bottom lip and tuck it in a little. Awe and lust were written all over her face. We both got a gleam in our eyes from the liquor and lust that was swarming inside of us. Each step I took across the room towards her felt heavy. My dick was so hard that I could feel the precum leaking from the tip.

"Era, you still want me to fuck you good baby?" I walked around her until my dick was up against her ass. She shuttered and nodded her head yes. With hooded eyes, I kissed her shoulder blades as I smoothly zipped her dress down, letting it fall down her sexy body. My mouth watered at the sight of her backside. *Got damn!*

The way her ass sat up was top shelf just like Roberto crazy ass had said. I could literally sit a two-litter soda bottle on the top of her ass, and it wouldn't dare fall. I bowed behind her and kissed each small roll of fat on her back then down to her ass cheeks. Her body smelled sweet like strawberries. Eyeing the black lace bra and thong, I removed both and made her bend over right in front of me.

The silence was appreciated, I needed it more than one would think. My drunken mind was irresponsible tonight and all I had been fantasizing hard on was how would she feel. Not being able to hold back, I push deep inside of her and stay still.

"What the fuck Era?" I pushed back then back in. "Like that baby?"

Her pussy was virgin tight, never in my life had I felt something so good. Shutting my eyes tight, I slid all the way out of her and made her turn around to face me. She gave me a nervous look as I slid my hands between her thighs and played in her wet folds. Shaking my head from side to side, I grab both of her perky heavy breasts and nibble on her chocolate drop nipples. Listening to her moan with need as her soft delicate fingers touch my shoulders, I release her nipples and we lock into an aggressive kiss.

Walking her backwards toward the bed, I take a seat and grab each ass cheek, guiding her to straddle me. Without being told, her eyes are low and heavy but locked in with mine. She eases down on my dick and keeps me deep inside of her rocking back and forth making sure to contract her pussy walls right on my dick. I spread each ass cheek like its giving me further access. I watch her intently as she repositions herself until she's in a squatting position, giving me no choice but to lay back and let her take control.

Her shoulder length straight hair is now sticking to her face, leaning forward her titties brush up against me. Era is fucking with my mind as she licks down my neck and bite a spot on the right side that makes me grunt and moan right into her mouth.

"You so fucking handsome, Soulful. I want you to take my soul tonight, just for this one night. I need this so bad." My hands are roaming her curvy body, it's so much body on top of me that I can't stop touching all over her. Smacking her on the ass, she starts to bounce up and down on my lengthy girth. I taste blood in my mouth, I bite down so hard that I'm causing myself pain mixed with the pleasure her pussy is giving me.

Biting my neck again, I realize that she noticed that it's a spot on me that makes me want to go ham in her pussy. I thrust upward meeting her halfway but feel like it's time for me to take control and fuck her until she's really hoarse and speechless.

Flipping our positions, I get between those milky smooth looking thighs and dip my head low until I'm tasting her sweet ass pussy. Her clit is throbbing with a pulse, and I make sure to lick it with enough pressure to make her legs shake.

Loving the way her flesh feels all over my tongue, I make sure to lick every crevice of her pretty ass pussy, until I smother my entire face in her center. Pulling an orgasm out of her was my goal, now it was time for me to put in that work.

I push my dick all the way inside of her not giving her a chance to recover, her body is spasming and convulsing right underneath me. Pussy was literally making all kinds of noises; I give her long ass strokes and nasty kisses. I wanted this shit to last forever but if I looked at the reality of what it was, we were doing right now then it'd make me go limp.

Looking down at my dick going in and out of her, she cries out and moans as she locks her legs around my waist. I love when the pussy creams on my dick and right now she had my entire dick soaked and coated with her sticky sweet essence.

"My pussy." I grunted as she sat up and licked my nipple, that shit had me stuck at first as I was still inside of her. She bit down on my nipple, and I moaned like a bitch as her pussy contracted again on my dick. Rotating her hips underneath me, she was fucking me back and that shit looked sexy as fuck.

"Fuck it, like it's yours daddy." She licked down the middle of my chest and tossed her arms around me. "Kill this pussy, Soulful." She sensually presses her thick lips against mine then push her tongue inside my mouth. My balls start to tighten as I go ham inside of her, I'm stroking so fucking hard that she falls back against the pillows and moans and whimpers as her body starts to tremble again. I can no longer hold back as I start emptying what feels like buckets of nut inside of her. Realizing that I was still deep inside of her, I pulled out and released what is left on her thigh.

"Got damn." I exclaimed and collapsed right next to her. We lay there silent; I feel numb and tired as fuck. My head started to pound as my heart seemed to be beating in my ears. I felt her move as she slowly stood on wobbly legs and walked towards the bathroom. I listen to Era pee then run sink water as my eyes start to get heavy. My plan wasn't to stay here but a fucked up part of me want more.

Era sauntered into the room, confidence leaking from her pores. The white towel in her hand as she approaches me, makes my dick twitch and I shake my head as I start to brick right back up at the sight of her luscious ass body. She timidly takes my dick and her free warm hand and uses the towel to clean up her juices off of me.

"Lick that shit off baby." Looking in my eyes with lust still evident, she lowered her mouth and lick on the head-first then engulf my entire dick into her mouth until I feel it knocking on her tonsils. My toes start to curl as she hums and moans on my dick while deep throating me like a fucking pro.

"Aww shit, Era!" I grab a handful of hair and guide her head up and down on my dick. No hands, no gagging, this shit was amazing how she could take all of my ten inches down her throat like it was nothing. Grabbing her breast, I tugged on her nipples. She looked me right in the eyes as she let me fuck her throat. I was on the verge of making a rookie-ass mistake and confessing some shit that I would regret when I was done so I tucked my lips into my mouth and grunted as she ate all my dick.

My phone started to ring from across the room, I eyed my pants knowing that's where my phone resided. I was on the verge of nutting, and I couldn't pull my dick out of her mouth to save my life right now. She sloppily sucked on the head of my dick then tapped it on the side of her face, rubbing the head of my dick all over her soft puffy lips she pushed me deep inside then made her throat tighten up around my shit and that was it for me. Era had me nutting down her throat while she guzzled me down without any leakage spilling from the sides of her mouth.

I wasn't done with her though, I got my breathing under control and got off the bed. Searching my pants pocket for my phone, I noticed it was Luv that I had a missed call from. I couldn't even be surprised that Jocelyn still hadn't called. Tossing my phone on the bed, I made a mental note to call Luv back in the morning.

Right now, I was enjoying the sight of Era on all fours with her swollen pussy lips on display. Saying nothing, I stood behind her and entered her from the back. Grabbing her waist, I pushed her back on my dick with no remorse. Fuck, this pussy was so damn good that I shouldn't have ever experienced this shit. It was lethal and dangerous as fuck. Hearing my phone ring again had me sighing hard, irritated as fuck.

Looking down at all the juices on my dick, I just can't pull out right now. The phone would have to wait. Era is on some straight sinister shit as she fucks me back unapologetically. I rise on my tippy toes and start making my dick do pushups deep inside her pussy. She reaches back and spread her ass cheeks far apart giving me a view of her tight asshole. I push a thumb inside her ass then switch my long strokes to short ones.

It looks like she's having a seizure on my dick she screams out that she's going to squirt, and I never experienced some shit like that, so I keep stroking as my phone keeps ringing. Era pleads for me to wait but there's no waiting with good pussy like this.

"Oh shit! Daddy! Soulful! Fuck!!!" she convulsed, and her pussy starts shooting out liquid the same way my dick shoots out nut. I rock in and out of her then pull out with my dick still oozing out nut. Her body twitches one last time before she collapses on her stomach with her ass still up in the air.

"Black fucking beauty." I look down at her moist damp body and lay down right next to her. I didn't give a fuck how saturated we had the bed, she had me weak in the fucking knees. My phone started to ring again and now reality was hitting me. Light snores escaped Era's lips; she looked so fucking sexy.

Finding the strength to roll over and grab my phone to answer, I don't even look at the caller I.D, I'm so high off of good ass sex that I don't see myself coming off the cloud. I needed this release; it had been long overdue.

"Oh my God! Teddy! Where are you!" The sound of Luv voice had me sobering up fast, I sat up as my mouth went dry. I had PTSD from the past when my mother was still living. Luv hadn't called me sounding like this in a long time.

"Luv? Talk to me." I nervously say just as I notice Era turning to her side to look at me.

"It's Jocelyn! Some nigga rang the doorbell and had her in his arms. She was passed out, he brought her in the house saying nothing and walked out. I thought it was weird, so I checked her to make sure she was at least alive like I used to do momma. Teddy her pulse was faint, I called the ambulance and now we are at Little Company of Hope." I shot up from the bed and went right to my clothes.

"What they saying Luv?" My voice croaked, a lump so thick forming into my throat as I feared for the worse.

"They saying its looking like she got a hold of some bad drugs." I dropped the phone as I looked around the room like some sick ass joke was being told to me. My wife? Drugs? Plus, a strange man coming to my fucking house? It felt like I was getting ready to explode.

Gathering myself, I stared at the phone on the floor in

disbelief, what the fuck did Luv just say to me about my wife? Picking the phone up and walking into the bathroom. I looked at myself in the mirror.

"Luv? You just said a stranger nigga brought my wife home off drugs and a possible overdose? He knows where the fuck we live and instead of taking her straight to the hospital he brings her half dead to the house?"

"Yes." Shaking my head, I let Luv know that I was on my way. I was worried about Jocelyn health but was also feeling vexed as fuck right now. Who the fuck was this nigga and how did he know where me and my wife lived at. I walked back into the room to put my clothes on. By the time I was done Era was sitting up wiping her eyes then looking up at me in confusion.

"I got to dip, some shit going down with my wife. You can sleep here, and I will have my driver scoop you in the morning." I looked at her and saw her face go through a series of different emotions. Now wasn't the time to play dumb, everybody knew that I was married so I didn't feel the need to tell her that before I fucked her.

"It's okay, I'll have a ride. Thank you for the good time Soulful." She got up and walked into the bathroom making me feel slighted. I walked up to the closed bathroom door and grabbed the door handle just as I heard shower water running. Twisting the knob, I was instantly rejected by it being locked. That was my sign right there to get the fuck out of this hotel and go see about my wife.

I shot Roberto a text telling him to meet me at the hospital; I shook the idea about texting anyone else and getting more parties involved. I decided to see how Jocelyn was first before calling her overbearing hating ass momma. On the way to the hotel, I logged into my home security monitoring system to get the image of whoever the nigga was that brought my wife home.

I paid a lot of money for my home security system to protect my family and keep an eye on things when I was on the road for games. My cameras had face recognition; anger consumed me as I played the video back multiple times studying the face of this dead ass nigga carrying my wife to my front door. My stomach knotted the fuck up when he leaned down and pecked her on the fucking lips. Zooming in, I noted the SGB tattoo on the center of his neck.

I was a street nigga before becoming a professional football player, this shit was about to get real because the nigga was from the Slaughter Gang Boys. First person I called was Debo, a nigga in his camp had to see me so I hoped that he was willing to pass the nigga over or I didn't have no problem going to war with slaughter gang or the blue diamond dynasty.

PRAYLAH

I woke up with a pounding headache and blurry eyes, feeling something tickle the inside of my thighs, I reached between my legs and grabbed a handful of dreads. My eyes landed on the ceiling fan in my room as I laid on my back and felt an intense sensation as a moan riped from my dry lips. Looking down right into those stone-cold gray eyes as Michael licked on my pussy like a dog drinking water from his bowl.

My legs are thrown over his shoulders as he sucked my sensitive flesh like he needed it. I become conscious of last night's events and why I'm lying in bed butt naked exposed not even having time to conceal my body. Michael and I didn't get a chance to have sex, we were so drunk that he took me home and made me strip down and get into the shower with him.

He bathed me from my neck down to my toes and then ate my pussy until I went hoarse and passed out right into his arms. I couldn't even think straight right now as he flattened his tongue then applied so much pressure to my clit that my body started to jerk.

"Uhhhhh!" I bite my bottom lip as I quiver hard and grab my breast into my hands and start pinching my nipples and rotating my hips to grind on his tongue harder. My breathing becomes shallow as the pressure starts to build up in my core. "Oh, Michael! I'm cuming baby." He grunted animalistic as he went harder.

Tears build up in my eyes as my muscles twitch and I start feeling an ache in the pit of my stomach. I thrust my hips forward riding the orgasm wave and his tongue with the precise way he was eating me. I cum so hard, I see stars and he just kept going in a tortuous way that kept my body jerking in shock and the sensitivity of my clit.

Reaching down I grab onto his dreads and massage his scalp as I beg him to stop.

"Let me catch my breath, Michael." I jerk off the bed a little as he chuckled lowly like he was not coming off of my pussy anytime soon. Clutching his dreads tighter, he finally eased up and started kissing my thighs and up my stomach then aligning his thick lips with mine. Kissing me hungrily made me feel hot all over. The taste of my pussy on his tongue made me want to fuck him now.

His massive hard body was wedged between my thighs, trailing my neck with his mouth leaving wet kisses. I'm lost in ecstasy a feeling I want to feel forever.

"Once I get inside of this pussy, it's mine forever. It doesn't matter if I fuck up or if you fuck up. You will belong to me." A chill crept down my spine as he entered me with a force that felt powerful. His eyes looked wild as he pumped into me with precision and power. I tilt my head back with my mouth agape. I felt Michael sucking on my chin as his callous hands crept underneath my back and then ran down to my butt, he grabbed a handful and squeezed tight.

Every time I brought my eyes to look into his, he was

staring intently never blinking, just giving me his full attention. Looking at his broad shoulders as he used my ass for leverage to push in and out of me was driving me insane. Running my hands through his soft locks as he punished my pussy, I hear him mumbling all kind of things under his breath.

His eyelids were heavy and low looking at me with those curly long natural lashes. Slowing down his fast strokes, he moved in and out of me slowly. Not knowing what to do with my hands, I caress down his back while I thrust back into his slow strokes. Sniveling and sweating, I started shaking again and he gave me a determined looked that said he already knew that I'm cumming on his dick.

I expected him to keep going but he didn't, he slid out of me and climbed off the bed. My eyes landed on his thick dick still glistening with my juices. He stood at the edge of the bed just watching me intently like he was trying to figure something out. The conflict shined bright into his eyes.

"You should let me meet your daughter real soon, I'm her dad now. I'm about to call my momma, give her this address so she can come talk to you. I think she can help you understand me better. Go shower and get dressed." He walked out of the room as I sat up still feeling high from our love making. That was very random and unexpected of Michael, but I was learning that it was how he operated.

I wasn't ready for him to meet Heaven and I didn't know if I was even ready for something serious. I felt our chemistry, but I was fresh out of a long and abusive relationship. I felt like I needed to see what it would be like being a single mother and providing for Heaven on my own.

Michael walked back into the room with his boxers on, I still sat in the middle of the bed confused. He got in the bed and laid his head back onto the pillow and closed his eyes.

"I'm taking those crazy pills. Shit gone make me fall asleep in a minute." He rubbed his large hand down his face as he sighed hard like he was frustrated.

"Umm Michael?" I cautiously called for his attention.

"Yea Pray?"

"I think we need to slow things down, I barely know you and it's the same for me with you." I wanted him to open his eyes to look me in mine but he kept his eyes shut.

"Doesn't matter, I know everything there is to know and I can learn more along the way. You belong to me now Praylah, once I slid inside of you, I discovered that I need you in order to breathe right. That's some deep ass shit ain't it?" He opened his eyes and looked into mine, every time our eyes connected it was something so fierce and deep.

His eyes moved me in a way that it felt spell bound, he didn't have to say much because his eyes had so much to say.

"I'll kill to keep you." He gave me an icy look and I knew he meant that in the literal sense which scared me to death.

"I think that's a bit much. I just got out of a relationship and I-"

"Stop talking Pray. I don't need to get mad right now." I got quiet and thought about all the times that Jarei tried to shut me up. I didn't like that I felt weak and unable to stand up for myself and make myself clearer. It's like I got Jarei comfortable with walking all over me and treating me wrong.

"If I make you mad… whats going to happen? I have every right to express myself and as a single woman that's just what I plan on doing." Michael offered me small snores, he already tapped out of the conversation that fast. I guess whatever medication that he was on really made him tired. I eyed his body, even with a limp dick tucked off in his briefs it was massive in size.

Getting up from the bed, I made my way into the bathroom to shower and get myself dressed for the day. After taking my medicine and throwing on a maxi dress, I slipped into my sandals and called my mom letting her know that I would be picking Heaven up around dinner time. My mom and dad asked to keep Heaven for one more day. I selfishly wanted to say no. I missed my baby and needed her close to me. I begrudgingly agreed to the extra day only because I felt like it was time for me to get the hell away from Michael.

A part of me didn't want to but I knew I needed time to just be alone and becoming dependent and accepting his help would mean that I would be under his control. He never brought up everything he was doing he really gave me my space. It had me bugging out and complaining because he didn't call or come around but now that we finally had sex and he was actually here saying all of these things, I was starting to become scared.

I called my best friend to see how her night went. It was very unlike her to leave the club with a stranger like she did last night. Although I was so focused on all the attention Michael was giving me last night. I could still see the chemistry that she and Soulful had.

"Hello?" She sounded groggy like she just woke up. I sat on the couch and kicked my feet up on the glass table. My body felt refreshed, and I was in a good mood besides the conversation that I tried to have with Michael.

"You want me to call you back?"

"Girl no, I needed to talk to someone anyway." I could hear Era readjusting herself.

"I fucked up Praylah." She sadly stated and I simpered right along with her.

"I fucked up too and I think me, and Heaven need to come live with you." I hated to impose but I didn't have anyone else. My parents would only be judgmental and if they did turn around and let me move back in with them. They would end up trying to control everything there was attached to me including the way that I raised Heaven.

"You know you don't even have to ask I want you guys to come here and live." A relief washed over me. I wanted to hop up now and go grab my keys and clothes and leave right now. I felt like I was speeding into a crash course with Michael and didn't want to experience more problems on top of the ones I already had.

"Thank you so much Era, you know I will give you some money on rent too. I have money saved since Michael hasn't asked me for any here."

"Girl please, just put food in the house and you can give me whatever you can on utilities. You got my God baby to take care of." I smiled at that, Era was always generous and caring.

"Thank you so much Era, I really appreciate you." She told me no problem and how I didn't have to thank her. Her voice sounded so sad and now I was curious to know what was bothering her so bad.

"Now tell me how you fucked up?" I was ready to hear this because Era always had things together. She never messed up things, it was always the opposite with her.

"I fucked a fine ass married man. I don't know why I didn't really look into him. I feel like a home wrecker. You know how I felt about Devin fucking on a bitch and here I am being the chick that messes with another woman's man. A married one at that." She sniveled, indicating that she was now crying.

"I was out of character for leaving with a random man. I actually loved every moment we spent together. The way he handled my body and our chemistry felt like we were on some love at first sight shit. It's so weird I can't even explain it Praylah. We fucked and went at it, he explored me, and I passed out. I woke up to him getting dressed and rushing out saying he needed to see about his fucking wife! I knew it was a one-night stand, but I thought we would be good friends or something. I was trying to convince myself of some things and get Devin out of my system totally, but I went about that shit the wrong way."

"It happens to the best of us. I mean look at me Era. I'm living in a place that our boss provided, catching feelings for a man I don't even know that well. The universe works in a weird way but what we can do is protect our hearts and get our shit together." We continued to talk, and I let her know that after I met with Michael's mom, I was going to stop by the grocery store to get us dinner and bring some wine so we could have a girls' night.

The car Michael had given me was in my name, so I would be taking that. I planned on leaving him the keys to his apartment and going on my way. I couldn't jump into something serious with him when I still had to face Jarei. I didn't want drama and man problems swirling around me and Heaven.

Hearing the doorbell ring, I let Era know that I'll be at her house in a couple of hours. I hung up and stood nervously to get to the door. Michael mom stood at the door at my same height with a beautiful woman that looked at me with an attitude.

"Hello sugar, my name is Kayori and this is a friend of Michael's, her name is Lakendra." The woman named Lakendra rolled her eyes and looked at me like she didn't want to be here. Kayori calling me sugar reminded me of how Michael called me sugar mommy.

"I'm Bo's ex-girlfriend." She offered a smirk, and I just nodded my head. I was used to dealing with attitudes because Jarei's baby momma Nyla always had one with me even when I was helping her out with her and Jarei's kid. I never argued with Nyla or came at her with resentment like most women would do. In my head it was Jarei's decision to cheat on me, so I didn't blame Nyla much.

I offered a welcoming smile and stepped to the side to let them in. Kayori surprised me, she didn't just walk by me like Lakendra did. She gave me a nice warm tight hug. I could see a small resemblance between her and Michael. Kayori was beautiful, the scars on her face complimented her and she wore them with confidence.

They both sat down as I went to the kitchen to bring them bottles of water.

"I was surprised that Michael called and asked for me to come and talk with you. He always keeps his personal life away from me and his father. What I'm here for is to give you good insight into who my son is. With Michael's father, I had to learn all about him including both of his personalities. I don't want to waste much time because I have to make sure my stubborn husband makes his four o' clock doctor appointment. Being with men like my husband and Michael requires a lot of patience." She cleared her throat and looked off for a second before she continued.

"Michael was diagnosed with schizophrenia paranoia as a kid. I believe he was around ten when we got the diagnosis. It's supposed to be a mild case but when he hit fifteen, they added obsessive-compulsive disorder and the list started growing. He has repetitive behaviors and compulsions that cannot be controlled by him, especially if he doesn't take his medications on a regular basis. Michael has his different phases, sometimes he won't sleep, eat properly or think rationally but he's very smart and loving to those he takes a liking to. He can be very over the top and sometimes he talks to himself a voice that's in his head that he gets frustrated over saying that it makes him do things he doesn't want to." Her eyes got watery as she looked me in the eyes.

"One of Michaels biggest mistakes and triggers was Lakendra." She eyed Lakendra and now Lakendra was looking remorseful. "It's a big reason why he refuses to totally move on from her. You see he regrets what he did to her and because of that he feels like he owes her, but he doesn't. Her sticking around waiting for him to offer her another chance should show him that Lakendra has forgiven him. She just wants to keep benefiting from-" Lakendra jumped up, I admired her slim thick curvy frame. She was a beautiful woman; my insecurities were soaring high. It made me wonder what Michael saw in me when he had this in fit beautiful model of a woman waiting for him.

"I love Michael! You think she can take care of your son the way that I'm willing to? Who the fuck is this fat bitch anyway! Bo does owe me! He owes us another try. This girl…" she spat in disgust as she pointed towards me. "Is just something to do until he's ready to come back around for me." I swallowed down hard, I felt slighted and jealous all in one as she chuckled nastily and looked down at me like I was truly a joke and I felt like one.

"Lakendra, sit the fuck down and speak at the same level that I am with you. I might be nice but baby I don't have it all when I feel disrespected. You and I both know how the fuck I get down. I'm trying to be nice but you're about to take me to a place called fuck you up." Kayori eyes turned into tiny slits as Lakendra quickly took a seat, eyes still on me.

"I fucked up, but no woman should have endured what I did. I regret not telling Michael sooner that it wasn't all his fault that night but because of his anger I didn't want to admit everything." Tears started falling from her eyes and even though she was disrespectful towards me. I felt bad for her. She eyed me with fiery emotion and anger as her lips quivered.

"Men like Debo think they have it all, for the most part they do except love. He's handsome, rich and got good dick. A young woman's dream. What women like me didn't know at a young age is what comes along with messing with a street nigga like Bo. They get to have bitches all kinds of bitches. Tall, short, fat, skinny, black or light skin. Hell, if he wanted to he could have a different bitch every single day of the year. It's all up to them and what they want. For the most part I dealt with Bo because now I'm still in love with him. It's nothing like having a street nigga that streets you like a fuckin Princess, he gave me whatever I wanted and made sure I was safe. He never let a soul disrespect me and if a nigga looked my way to long, he'd knock them where the hell they stood. I loved that shit, it's like an addiction, a rush, and thrill. As time went by, Bo started acting differently. He'd fuck up from time to time and admit to me by telling the truth. Never would he fuck a bitch but if he was away and out of town, I agreed that it was fine for him to get head from a random bitch here and there if I wasn't there to fulfill his needs. As long as none of them bitches came around bragging about it. There was a bitch named Tashay from my hood going around with a baby bump saying the baby belonged to Bo. That shit fucked me up bad, I'm talking the kind of pain that puts you into so much shock, grief and hurt." She grabbed her chest like someone had punched her in it.

"Of course, I confronted Bo about it, and he denied it. Looked me right in the eyes and denied it. I should've believed it but my insecurities and the way I felt at the time didn't allow me to believe. I acted as if I did and the whole time, I was plotting to hurt him like he hurt me." She eyed Kayori cautiously as Kayori seemed to be upset and agitated with the whole story telling from Lakendra.

"I end up fucking one of his slaughter gang boys and I got pregnant by him. I continued to mess with him since he made me feel good, he was on call whenever I missed Bo a little too much. Months went by and I didn't stop what I was doing until I got to comfortable and lazy with it. Bo was excited about going out of town with Ream and Solo, so I got bold and let Doughboy come to Bo and I house. I guess Bo had Ream tell his pilot to hold off so he could double back to the house for his favorite chain that I overlooked on the dresser. I had been so excited to lay up with Doughboy that if I saw Bo's chain on the dresser then I would have instantly known that Bo was coming back. I didn't realize that because every time I laid up with Doughboy, I felt myself getting redemption and even with Bo for all the hoes he had gotten head from, I felt like it was fair, and I made myself believe that he had gotten another bitch pregnant."

"How you getting even when you told my son that you were okay with getting head from other hoes! On top of that he made the same girl that claimed she was pregnant tell you that she had lied, and the baby wasn't his. You just wanted to cheat! I'm not gonna sit here and let you tell this story and try to justify your foul ass actions!" Kayori cut Lakendra off, but I wanted to hear the rest of her story.

"I'm sorry, I was wrong, but Bo was still wrong for what he did." She sobbed out and wiped at the tears that couldn't seem to stop flowing. "He had to know that I didn't want him with any other hoes not even head! If he loved me enough, he would have never even taken me up on my offer!"

"Finish the got damn story Lakendra because I was under

the impression that the baby was Michael's this whole time." Lakendra now looked nervous, but she continued to tell the story.

"Bo walked in on me and Doughboy, we were in the living room making out like teenagers. My gown was up, and Doughboy was playing with my pussy. So caught up in fore-play I didn't even hear Bo enter the door even if I did it would look to weird with Doughboy being there. The only thing that got my attention was Bo emptying the clip in Doughboy's head. Blood... blood and brain matter all over me." Her hands shook as she held herself. "I never seen Bo so angry, it was the first night I heard and saw him conflicted, pacing back and forth before he acknowledged me. He was talking to himself and hitting his head with his gun until he busted his head. He kept yelling out that he couldn't kill me because he loved me too much and how he fucked around too. Then he turned to face me, it was as if I was looking into a stranger's eyes. His eyes were wild and crazed. He charged me like a football player and was beating my face in until I yelled out that he was going to kill our baby. It's like he snapped back into reality and the Bo I knew came back to the forefront. He left the house and had his boys clean up the mess that he made. I didn't see Bo for three weeks; he only came to me after I texted him saying how I was in the hospital suffering from a miscarriage at almost five months pregnant. Bo always talked about having kids, so he was crushed thinking that our baby had died because of him putting hands on me." She broke down and cried into the palms of her hands.

"You mean to tell me I killed another nigga baby? That baby was never even mine Lakendra." Michael stepped into the room, his voice super raspy and deep like he had just woken up. Hurling his phone at the wall and pulling his gun from his waist, he cracked his neck from side to side and stared hard at Lakendra. He mumbled some shit under his breath and started pacing in front of us. Kayori his mother stood and went to her son, and he roared loud causing me to jump.

"MOVE!" Kayori stayed calm and grabbed her son by the face.

"I won't move! I know that voice is trying to control you baby, but you can't let it. You needed to hear it MICHAEL! You didn't kill a baby she miscarried, and the baby wasn't yours. You have to stop holding on to Lakendra out of guilt and let her move on. Things happen for a reason and that's my reasoning for bringing Lakendra here today. Take deep breaths baby like Ms. Scott told you the other week. Breathe baby, breathe." He listened to his mom then his eyes landed on me.

"I guess I'm too crazy to deal with now? I guess you over there judging me. Well, I don't give a fuck. Get your shit and go, all of you bitches is the same! Except you momma, you probably the last real one left, daddy lucky to have you." He bent down and placed his forehead onto his mom's forehead.

"Lakendra and Praylah get the fuck out before I lay one of y'all down in front of my momma. I don't want to disrespect my momma."

"Relax sugar." She rubbed his shoulders like she was trying to tame a beast. I didn't waste any time, I got up and grabbed my keys and purse then left.

I looked at Michael one last time and saw resentment and hurt in his eyes. It looked like he wanted to stop me from leaving and I wanted to stop myself from leaving. I left anyway feeling sad for him and me, Michael had made a mistake. He beat himself up over it and today he found out some things that he didn't know. I said a silent prayer as I got into my car. I prayed for his sanity and the mental space he was currently in. I would be here for him but as far as a serious relationship I couldn't give him that. We both had problems when it came to our mental. That alone could be explosive and toxic all in one.

DEBO

"Nigga, why you driving behind the pigs so damn fast! Slow this bitch down!" I looked over at Honor and smirked. She had her feet pressed all hard against the passenger side floor like she was on the driver's side. It looked like she was trying to push down on imaginary brakes. Holding on to her seat belt tight she looked over at me like she was scared. Shit was comical as fuck, I accelerated higher and sped up.

"Chill the fuck out, they going fast, so I'm going the same speed as them. How can they pull me over when I'm behind them. They speed I speed." I turned the music up and switched lanes, following what the cops did. I was in a rush to go break a niggas face in.

Niggas knew that Honor was my General, head bitch in charge. I had too much going on mentally, legally and illegally to hold niggas nuts and guide them along the way.

"You know I handled that nigga, right?" Honor turned my music down. "Why the fuck you keep playing this old slow ass song." I shrugged off her question. Smokey Robinson's "The Agony For The Ecstasy" was one of my favorite songs.

I usually listened to the shit to calm my nerves. My dad put me on to it when I was a young nigga.

"You a female, and my General. If a nigga put hands on any female that I rock hard with. Don't matter if they look like a nigga or a fucking termite, he gone have to answer to me." I tightened my grip on the steering wheel.

Honor could hold her own; she was as lethal as me when it came to running shit. It's just that niggas had a hard time adjusting and following her direction because she was indeed a female. Honor kept shit organized and she stayed on niggas necks making sure they didn't slack.

"I'm saying it's good because for the past two weeks you been acting unhinged as fuck. I normally call meetings for the gang, so you don't have to waste time, Debo. You can possibly go up in this muthafucka killing more of our men that we actually need right now." She passed me the blunt that she damn near sucked down. I took it, I needed something potent to get my mind right. I stopped taking percs because I noticed when I was fucking on Praylah, I couldn't bring myself to nut even though I wanted to.

"I ain't that cold." I picked my phone up in the middle console and answered it.

"Alesia, what's good?" I blew smoke from my nose already knowing my assistant was about to give me an ear full.

"Nigga don't what's good me." She spoke low into the phone. "I need you here at the office no later than Friday or I'm coming to find you. There's paperwork that you need to sign off on and the board would like to present some things to you."

It was good owning shit and being a businessman. It was all the foot work and signing off on shit then sitting in long ass meetings with tight ass suits that got on my fucking nerves.

"Sign off on the shit, Alesia damn! I got other things that need my attention. Tell the board I'm not open to new ideas or projects right now." I hit the blunt again and pulled into an alley. This nice ass two story house on the Eastside of LA looked like a nice cozy family home from the outside. Niggas from around the way knew it served as headquarters. I had shit built underneath this home that nobody knew about except Ream and Solo and now Honor.

"This is not up for debate, Debo. I handle everything so you won't have to show face as much. Remember this is your company and it requires your time and attention. If you want-"

"Somebody to kiss your ass and do your job… find another slave assistant." I finished her sentence because she loved trying to fake threaten me. "Yea I hear you light bright. I'll see yo thick ass Friday. Twerk something for a nigga and make it worth my time since you so desperate to see me." She started cursing and yelling, I hung right up in her face. Alesia's ass stayed having a mini heart attack about my company. That's why I gave her the position, she went above and beyond and kept shit multiplying.

"Remind me to send her crazy ass a flower arrangement today and a spa card. They over there stressing her." I tapped the top of my glove compartment and Honor opened it passing me my nine-millimeter.

"What's up with that nigga Sosa?" I asked before getting out of the car. The sun in Cali was shining hard, I reached back in my Maserati and grabbed my Balenciaga glasses. Opening up the back door, I snatched up my white Balenciaga shirt and threw that on next. I didn't want any wrinkles in my shit.

"Niggas looking for him." Honor walked around the car and gave me an, *I told you so* look. I scanned the backyard and frowned at empty bottles of liquor and cups scattered on the grass.

"I told you what the nigga was gone do. He did good with the first two bricks, gave the nigga four of them birds and now he a week late."

"A week late?" I calmly asked, that made Sosa no longer someone I called a homie. What's crazy is I'd off a nigga for being a day late with my money. Four bricks of yae were worth his life. Just one brick could put a nigga on, especially after a nigga stepped on it and broke it down. My shit was pure as fuck. I normally sold my shit for twenty-one thousand a brick, but gave Sosa a deal, that was fifteen thousand a brick.

"Yo veins popping out yo neck Hulk smash." Honor tried to play it light, but I didn't give a fuck about her dry ass jokes. I bit on my bottom lip to calm myself; I felt like exploding. *See, you always need me to guide yo dumb ass! I told you about this nigga!* Shaking my head to rid myself of that voice, I picked up my size ten foot and kicked the back gate in, knocking it flat on the grass.

"Aye Debo, calm yo ass down Blood!" Honor was right behind me trying to calm me with words that I ignored.

"Don't tell me to calm down, Honor. Make the call and locate that nigga. I want him found in under an hour." I knocked on the back door and one of my young goons on door duty opened up with an AK in his hands.

"Go clean the front and back fuckin' yard nigga." I marched past him and walked into the front room. As far as I was concerned, I didn't have much time to be here. That's why I kept my car running so I could do what I had to do and jump right back into my whip and leave.

Entering the room, I chuckled lowly as I eyed every nigga acting frantic when they were just smoking and lounging around. Money was scattered along with empty food containers. I turned around and looked at Honor, her face mirrored mine. Looking at her swollen lip reminded me of why I was here.

I looked over at Dmack and nodded my head at him.

"Honor, why you and this nigga Dmack get into it?" I calmly asked as she stood next to me. I already knew what happened and I believed Honor over all of these niggas. I just wanted to see what his bitch ass had to say.

"Debo, that bitch be tripping. Treating niggas like-" I shook my head no and he stopped talking. See I was a different kind of disrespectful nigga, some would call it ignorance. I lived up to every word that a person had to say bout me. Niggas like Dmack was fake and snake as fuck. I had been waiting on a reason to justify my actions by killing this bitch ass nigga.

"See that? How another man can shut you the fuck up right on que? Treating you like the pussy ass nigga you is?" I tilted my head, and he balled his face up.

"What nigga? You ain't a pussy? Cause hitting on some pussy seems real fishy." I chuckled and stepped a little closer to him.

"If you ain't a pussy stand the fuck up nigga and prove to us that you not a pussy." I removed my gun from my waist and gave it to Honor.

"I respect you too much Debo, I ain't on that my nigga. Honor just be talking to niggas like she some superior ass bitch. Niggas moving weight and working day in and day out. She wanna get mad cause niggas decide to throw a lil get together the other night." My phone pinged and I checked my message. It was from Soulful, a picture with this niggas

Dmack face right on my screen holding Soulful wife. Seconds later another text came through with Dmack kissing Soulful's wife lips while she appeared limp.

I called Soulful right away to get some clarification on the situation.

"I'm standing right in front of the nigga now, what's good baby boy?" I got right to it soon as Soulful answered.

"Ask him how the fuck does he know Jocelyn Hurtz?"

"Jocelyn Hurtz, how the fuck you know her and why was she in your arms passed out? Be real specific." I eyed him not really liking how this shit was gone end up panning out.

"She my lil bitch that be putting me on at the clubs and shit. She be off that yae and I told her to be easy on it. We went out partying, I brought her back here and we finished the night turning up. She had some yae but claimed she got that shit from the other side, from the getting money niggas." His hands start shaking and he was looking everywhere around the room at his boys like someone was going to save him.

"That shit had fenti in it." Soulful said into the phone.

"We don't do fenti in my product." My jaw clenched because not only was Sosa stomping down hard on the product that I was giving him. He was lacing the bricks with Fentanyl.

"He know where I live, he violated." Soulful added and I nodded my head but said nothing.

"It's handled nigga."

"Bet." He hung up, I turned and took my gun from Honor and aimed it right at Dmack, he tried to duck and move but I was too fast. Two to the dome, brains in his lap. My eyes scanned the room wildly.

"For any of you niggas getting this shit confused and fucked up, let me make this shit clear. Honor is you niggas general. You either honor that or get laid the fuck down. On some real slaughter gang shit, I been nice. Letting niggas breathe and ya baby motha's twerk. Don't ever take my nice and calmness for some shit you think you will be able to handle. I'm still really like that, the same nigga that make momma's wear all black with big glasses and hats to shield all that mourning they gone be doing for life."

I eyed every nigga in the room to see which one of these niggas wanted to step up and have some shit to say. Dmack was too mouthy, always trying to appear like he was big and bad when he ain't never put in no major work.

"If you don't like the way the get down is then disappear before I make you disappear. This shit ain't daycare or school. Ain't no bringing hoes to the spot, no partying here, and I bet not ever come around this bitch seeing my shit dirty like this again. The same way you act with me is how you act with Honor." I nodded my head at Honor, and we walked towards the back to leave.

"Clean this bitch down and get rid of that nigga." It wasn't even my intention to kill a nigga today, but Dmack had violated Soulful. If it was my wife and my house, I would want a nigga to act on it if I wasn't able to get to the situation.

Soon as I got in the car my mind went to Praylah, I wanted to see about her real bad. That shit with Lakendra had fucked me up bad. All these years, I kept taking care of Lakendra because I was under the impression that I was the reason behind her losing our baby. That shit haunted me bad, night and day. Beyond all the bullshit, I really was in love with Lakendra at one point.

She had a lot of selfish ways, but she was the woman that I had fallen for and I over looked a lot of shit like she did with me. I didn't play her as bad as she thought, I never stuck my dick in a bitch but her when we were together. Lakendra let other hoes get in her head about me, when she should have been believing me and what I was telling her.

My father didn't play that shit when it came to honesty. He taught me and all my siblings to stand on everything that came out of our mouths. He couldn't stand a liar; he was always brutally honest and didn't give a fuck who feelings he hurt. I was the same way; I came off as blunt and mean but I always told the truth even when I didn't really want to.

Lakendra lying was the worst thing she could have done besides fucking another nigga in my home. I was a hundred percent sure that she had her foul ass still at my house. I hadn't addressed her or gone around her in two weeks hoping that she saved herself from the embarrassment. To be real I didn't need any more closure from her, and she didn't need any from me.

All Lakendra needed to do was move the fuck around and get the fuck up out my spot. By now she had enough money and nice things from me from over the years to get on with all her shit.

"So much for you not killing anyone." Honor mumbled under her breath as she started breaking down some weed inside of a hundred-dollar bill.

"Nigga had it coming, he violated with Soulful." I unlocked my phone just as I turned out of the alley and drove around to the front of the house to make sure them niggas was cleaning the front lawn like I had instructed. I didn't want to bring no negative attention to the two-story family home. We didn't have a lot of traffic here, it was a place to count up, cook up and move shit the fuck out.

I even had my homegirl Tashane living there with her ghetto ass sisters to make that shit believable. Them niggas throwing a party against my wishes really had me ready to lay them all out but at the same time I understood how shit went.

When I was young and getting money, I never followed no niggas orders. I did my own thing and did that shit well. The only difference was, I was a cold devil with my shit.

I bullied the bullies and the niggas that thought that they could take me on I laid them the fuck out too. The only niggas I never tried to disrespect or overstep was my father and my uncle Stone. I'd be lying if I said that sometimes both of them niggas made me want to test the waters and get with their asses too. The only thing with that was I knew that my dad was just as nutty as me but fuckin worse. You tempt the Beast, and all his demons would start spilling out. The only person that could tame him was my mother.

Once I peeped shit out, I chuckled at the frowns plastered on these grown niggas faces as they picked trash up from the front lawn. Going to my messages, I clicked on Praylah's name and went to our thread. I texted and called her one too many times and wasn't feeling how she was curving me. She never came back to the spot that I gave her, and I didn't like that shit.

It had me wondering if she took her ass back to her punk ass baby daddy. I even checked my time sheet at Beastly Cravings from the website I had set up by Alesia. She had been going to work and from the cameras, she was still driving the car. So, my only question was where the fuck had she been staying. My only answer came back around to her dumb ass being posted back up at the house that she shared with that bitch ass baby daddy of hers.

I didn't give a fuck how mad I got that day, she had to understand that a nigga was just locked deep into my feelings. Finding that bullshit out about Lakendra and how tough she had played me had me thinking all kind of fucked up things about women in general.

I pulled closer to the curb and got out and walked to the

passenger side just as Honor was sealing the blunt. Telling her to drive towards Praylah's old spot, I got comfortable in the passenger seat as I called Praylah's phone blocking my number so she couldn't see that it was me calling.

"No, no Heaven! Sit down and watch Cocomelon for you get a pop pop!" I listened to Praylah's sexy ass voice, and my heart did some weird shit.

"Umm, hello?" She gave me her attention and for a couple of seconds I didn't know what to say.

"You cheating on me Sugar mommy?" I licked my top row of teeth and leaned my seat back, resting my head against the head rest. Sparking up the blunt, I looked over at Honor who was big cheesing and mouthing the words "Simp ass" to me as I flicked her ass off.

"How can I cheat on you when we not even together, Michael?" I could hear the slight attitude in her voice, shit had my dick getting hard. Since I hadn't been taking those damn percs, I was ready to bust a long overdue nut.

"There you go talking all that ditzy ass shit. Fuck I tell you when I slid all inside of that sugar cane?" I smirked at hearing her breathing all hard into the phone. I could just imagine the nervous look that she was sporting on her face. Hitting the facetime option, she accepted. I remained silent as I stared into her pretty ass face. Her cheeks were turning red as she kept blushing and smiling into the phone and a nigga wasn't even saying shit yet.

She had her face so close to the phone that I couldn't see her background. I wasn't tripping though, cause I had the perfect idea of where her ass was at. I was about thirty minutes away from her with gay ass butterflies in my stomach. This feeling she gave me was some shit that I wanted to feel for forever, so I needed to secure it fast.

"That was a bunch of sex talk Michael. We both have too

much going on to be trying something serious. I think we need to be friends, get to know each other better and learn each other's triggers."

"I ain't going for that, Praylah. You mine, you hear me sugar?" Honor started chuckling, I probably sounded like an old ass man. Honor didn't really need to know the real reasoning behind me calling Praylah sugar.

"I'm serious Michael, I still have to figure things out with Heaven's dad. I want a healthy co-parenting relationship with him. I don't want any drama." I pulled at my beard hairs and nodded my head. Praylah didn't know just how deep she was in with me. I'd let her believe whatever bullshit came to her mind about us. I knew what it was and what it wasn't going to be.

"Why you over there at that house Praylah." Her eyes grew big as fuck, shit was funny how timid, shy and scared Praylah was.

"I'm gathering some things for Heaven and I. I will now be living with my best friend Era." I got pissed a little but reminded myself that Praylah was trying to be on some fake independent shit since she was done with her bitch ass baby daddy.

"Yea alright, I'm fenna fall through. Meet my step-daughter and shit." She shook her head no fast before she could get the words out. I looked out the window and saw that we were about ten minutes away from her old house.

"No, Michael don't do that. I don't want to start anything; Heaven's dad should be home in another hour to visit with her and I know you showing up would just make things uncomfortable." Her voice sounded choppy, and she looked like she was stressed out. I didn't like how this nigga had Praylah so fucking scared. It was time for me to meet and beat the nigga that called himself putting hands on a fucking female.

"It's time that I meet that nigga anyway. You ain't seen the nigga in a while and I'll be damned if he tries to put his hands on you again. Like I said I'm on the way." I hung up in her face and put my phone on silent. She was already blowing my phone up and sending text to stop me from coming. Praylah would learn real fast the way that her man got down.

"You can't bully that girl or her baby daddy, Debo." Honor took the blunt from me and I looked at her with a face that said *really?*

"I would never bully Praylah but that baby daddy of hers gone get it all. I'm knocking that nigga back just off the strength of him putting his hands on Praylah. If that nigga get too disrespectful then I'm going to body him. Feel me?" We pulled onto Praylah's street.

"No nigga and listen to me now. If you really digging her and want her in the way that you claim. You better be easy on that wanting to kill her baby daddy. No matter how dirty the nigga did her, she still love that nigga and after all its her child's father. You kill him and she might just snitch or better yet really be done with yo crazy ass." I thought about what Honor said and knew it was true.

I never found myself in a situation like this before, I usually didn't consider other people feelings when it came to killing a nigga. With Praylah I did, I was willing to accept all of her baggage including her daughter. Now the shit had me thinking tough, because Praylah was a square and it was clear that she wasn't used to all the killing and hood shit that I was on. I was still her boss after all and had to consider that shit too.

Honor pulled up to the curb and I hopped out and tucked my gun in my waist. Checking my surroundings, I strolled up to the porch and tapped on the door twice. Praylah snatched the door open with wide panic-stricken eyes and looked at me in horror. Ignoring all that shit I took a couple of seconds to admire her from head to toe.

Her red hair was curly back in that fro hiding most of her face. She didn't have on any make up, so her face looked a little paler than usual like she hadn't been in the sunlight. Jealously crept over me as I stared at the shape and outline of her curves and the skintight black leggings she had on. Her camel toe looked heavy as fuck sitting upright in her leggings. I eyed the Nikes sports bra and looked up at her like she was crazy.

Praylah pretty ass had too much ass and curves to be dressed the way that she was.

"You tryna get that old thing back or something Pray?" I cocked my head to the side as she shook her head no fast.

"What? No! I told you that I'm moving my things, Michael." I pushed back her mass of curls to see her full face. Pulling her by the chin then kissing her on the cheek on top of that pretty ass colorful birthmark plastered on her cheek, I grabbed a handful of ass and stuck my tongue down her throat.

Giving her a couple of seconds to breathe and look at me with now heavy-lidded eyes, I pecked her again on the lips.

"I'm here to help you move and meet my stepdaughter, sugar mommy. Is that okay with you?" I pushed my hand between her thick thighs and cupped her fat ass pussy.

"Ye- yes Michael that's fine, we just have to be quiet. Ummm Heaven just went down for a nap." She moaned as I cupped her pussy tighter making sure that I applied more pressure.

"Why you telling me all of that? You want me to beat this fat ass pussy up? It's wet for me sugar mommy?" She moaned softly right into my mouth as I licked around her top and bottom lip. I pulled her bottom lip with my teeth and bit down a little with my eyes on hers loving the way they rolled back. She took steps backwards letting me into the house.

I shut the door with my foot not wanting to take my hands off of her soft body.

"I think you make me more fucking crazy in the head Pray. That shit ain't good baby." I picked her up off her feet and walked her towards the room since her baby was on the couch sleep. "I need to feel you, like I gotta bury and print myself deep inside you baby." I licked on her neck; she smelled so fucking good. Once we got in the room I tugged at her legging and made sure to pull her panties down along with her leggings.

"Michael, I haven't taken a shower since early this morning." She covered her pussy like I hadn't already seen it.

"I love your dirty drawls baby. I don't give a fuck if the pussy got a little must to it, that's my pussy, plus it just means that it's been marinating all day for a nigga." She giggled turning red and shit. Just as I was preparing to pull my dick out of my pants, I heard the sound of a gun clicking behind my head and Praylah screaming at the top of her lungs.

"Jarei please! It's not what you think." I smiled and winked at her, feeling this niggas hot breath on my neck. I turned and was surprised to see this bitch ass nigga that owed me money with a gun to my face.

"Sosa? Oh yea, it's just what you think nigga. Now put that gun down before you hurt yo self."

To be continued...

KEEP IN TOUCH

Subscribe

Interested in keeping up with more of my releases? To be notified first of all my upcoming releases and sneak peeks, please subscribe to my mailing list! https://bit.ly/3AYIwMK

Contact me on any of my social media handles as well!

Facebook- Authoress Masterpiece & Masterpiece Reads

Facebook private group for updates- Masterpiece Readers

Instagram- authoress_masterpiece & masterpiece_lgee

Email – masterpiece3541@outlook.com

Made in the USA
Middletown, DE
05 July 2023

34598475R00097